THE BELT OF SEVEN TOTEMS

KIRK MONROE

(Frontispiece by John Betancourt.)

THE BELT OF SEVEN TOTEMS

A Story of Massasoit

KIRK MUNROE

WILDSIDE PRESS

INTRODUCTION

Massasoit Sachem, or Ousamequin (1581–1661), was the sachem or leader of the Wampanoag confederacy. "Massasoit" means "Great Sachem."

This novel was not intended as a true recreation of Pilgram-era history; instead, it is the author's attempt to reconcile apparently conflicting historical facts and to explain an otherwise inexplicable situation concerning Native Americans and European settlers. At the time of the Pilgrims, all Native Americans—not excepting those of New England—had suffered repeated outrage at the hands of white men, and in no case had they been given any cause to love the invaders of their country or to welcome their presence. Why, then, did the powerful Massasoit permit a white invasion of his territory that he could so easily have crushed?

Clearly a strong friendship existed from the very first between him and Edward Winslow, and Winslow seems to have exercised a great influence over the New England sachem. What was the origin of this friendship? The Narragansetts, while submitting to Massasoit's authority, were always in sullen opposition to it. Why? It is to answer these questions that Kirk Monroe constructed this tale, and he advances a convincing theory through it.

A modern reader less familiar with the era should note that many New England natives were kidnapped and taken to Europe. The wampum belt, on which was pictured the distinguishing totems of seven leading New England clans, was worn by both Massasoit and Metacomet (King Philip), his son, and is still in existence. Tasquanto (Squanto) was kidnapped from Cape Cod and taken to England, where he remained for several years. Captain Dermer carried a number of native Americans to London, where he sold them to be exhibited as curiosities. (He finally died of wounds received at the hands of Native Americans in New England.) Champlain did aid a war-party of Hurons to defeat the Iroquois in one instance, and in another was defeated by the same foe. Although there is no record of it, might not Massasoit have been among those taken to Europe?

While this story is admittedly fictional, it does have a substantial historical basis. Interested readers can learn more about Massasoit in Alvin G. Weeks' book, *Massasoit of the Wampanoags* as well as other histories of Native American people.

—Karl Wurf
Rockville, Maryland

CHAPTER I

THE VILLAGE OF PEACE

In the olden days when the whole land belonged to the red man the village of Longfeather the Peacemaker was located on the river of Sweet Waters, nearly one hundred miles, as the crow flies, from the place where it flows into the sea. Its ruler was Longfeather, the only son of Nassaup, sachem of the Wampanoags, and a man wise enough to realize that peace was better for his people than war. So he had sent his only son, when still a mere youth, to one after another of the surrounding tribes that he might learn their language and establish friendships among them. Thus Longfeather had lived for months at a time among all the tribes dwelling east of the Shatemuc and the country of the terrible Iroquois. He had travelled as far north as the land of the Abenakis, from whom he learned to make snow-shoes and to construct canoes of birchen bark. He had visited the Nipmucks and Nausets of the eastern coast, who taught him many secrets of the salt waters from which they gained their living. He had journeyed to the southward, spending a year with the Narragansetts and another with the Pequots, the wampum-making tribes. Then for a long time he had remained with the warlike Mohicans, whose great chieftain Tamenand loved him as a son, and taught him from his own wisdom until Longfeather became wisest of all Indians dwelling in the region afterwards known as New England.

So many seasons of corn-planting and harvest did the youth spend in travel and study among the tribes, that when he finally turned his face towards his own people he was become a man in years as well as in stature and strength. So it happened that he tarried again among the Pequots until he had won for a bride Miantomet, a daughter of their sachem. The principal industry of this tribe being the production of wampum, which was made in the form of cylindrical beads, white, black, purple, and sometimes red, cut from sea-shells, Longfeather's bride was presented with a vast store of this precious material in the form of strings and belts, so that in winning her the young man also acquired much wealth.

To fittingly celebrate the home-coming of his son, Nassaup commanded a great feast that should last for seven days, and to it were invited the headmen of all the tribes in which Longfeather had made friends. The place chosen for this notable gathering was the mouth of a beautiful valley, centrally located for the convenience of the several tribes, and gently sloping to the river of Sweet Waters. Here, then, in early autumn, at the full of the harvest moon, were gathered hundreds of the leading sannups of the wide-spread territory bounded by the great white river (St. Lawrence) on the north, the salt waters that bathe the rising sun on the east and south, and the Shatemuc (Hudson) on the west. These, together with their families, formed an assemblage larger and more important than any that could be recalled even by tradition, and while much of their time was devoted to feasting and dancing, they also discussed questions of great significance.

One of these was the meaning of a vast ball of fire, that, brighter than the sun and glowing with many colors, had shot athwart an evening sky on the night of Longfeather's marriage to Miantomet. To some this phenomenon portended evil, while to others it was an omen of good promise; but all were convinced that it was connected in some way with the fortunes of Longfeather.

Another matter discussed early and late with unflagging interest was the rumored appearance in remote regions of a race of beings having human form, but unlike any heretofore known. They were said to have white skins and hairy faces, and were believed to control thunder and lightning, which they used for the destruction of all who came in their way. Some of them were also described as bestriding fire-breathing monsters of such ferocity that they carried death and destruction wherever they went. Most of these rumors came from the south and from lands so remote that they had been many months travelling from tribe to tribe and from mouth to mouth. Whether the beings thus imperfectly described were gods or devils none could tell. At the same time those who heard of them agreed that in spite of their form they could not be human, for were not all men made in one likeness, with red skins, black hair, and smooth faces?

It was disquieting that, while most of these rumors came from the far-distant south, some of them also came from the north, and located the white-skinned strangers not more than a month's journey away. At the same time it was comforting to have all stories agree that, while they appeared from the ocean borne on the backs of vast winged monsters of the deep, they always, after a while, disappeared again as they had come.

Longfeather further reassured those who discussed these matters by relating a tradition that he had received from Tamenand. It concerned other supernatural visitants who had once come even to the land of the Wampanoags; but so long ago that not even the great-grandfather of the oldest man living had seen them. They also were described as of white skin and having hair on their faces. It was not told that they rode fire-breathing dragons, or that they were armed with thunderbolts, but they had come from the sea and returned into it again when they were ready for departure. To be sure, they had slain many of the native dwellers and caused great fear throughout the land, but after going away they had never again been seen. To this day, however, traces of their visitation remained in the form of certain pictured rocks that they had inscribed, and which no man might remove or even touch, under penalty of death.

The simple-minded forest-dwellers listened to these tales with the same dread that would inspire us of to-day upon hearing that inhabitants of some distant planet, bringing death-dealing weapons that were unknown to us, had invaded the world. They shuddered, gazing furtively about them as they listened, and drew closer together as though for mutual protection. Although the fears thus aroused sobered the red-skinned assemblage and left it in small humor for further festivities, this was not regretted by Nassaup, since it rendered them the more willing to listen to a plan that he wished to propose. It was one so long considered that it had become the chief desire of his life, and was nothing more nor less than a federation of all the tribes there represented, in the interests of peace, mutual aid, and protection. For two days was this proposition discussed, and then it was accepted. A belt of wampum, on which was worked his own totem, was given to each of the seven head chiefs present, and a great belt of the same material, in which the seven totems were combined, was presented to Longfeather. On account of his wisdom he had been unanimously chosen to rule the allied tribes, and this Belt of Seven Totems was the badge of his authority. So Longfeather became Peacemaker and Lawgiver to all that region, and on account of its central location he established his official head-quarters upon the very spot where the great assemblage had been held. Thus was founded the village of Peace, in which all questions affecting relations between the tribes were discussed and treaties were made. It was a place of refuge to which all persons accused of wrong-doing and in danger of their lives might flee, with a certainty of protection until their cases could be considered by the Peacemaker. It also became a trading-point to which were attracted the skilled makers of such articles as were most in demand among the tribes.

Large areas of nearby lands were brought under cultivation, and these, fertilized with fish taken in quantities from the teeming river, produced wonderful crops of beans, maize, and pumpkins. No war-parties ever visited the village of Peace, but there was a constant coming and going of strangers. To it travelled the Abenakis, bringing furs, maple-sugar, and highly prized ornaments of copper that had come to them from the far west. Here they exchanged these things for bales of dried fish from the eastern coast, seal-skins, or belts of wampum. Here, also, they found expert makers of flint arrow-heads, knives, and hatchets, weavers of mats, and workers in clay, from whom they might procure rude vessels of earthen-ware.

Above all, here dwelt Longfeather, to whom could be submitted all dis-puted questions, with a certainty that he would settle them wisely and justly. Thus it happened that the village of Peace became the political capital and chief trading-point of all New England long before ever a white man had set foot in that region. Here, too, some twenty years after its founding, was born Nahma, the son of Longfeather, a lad whose strange adventures in after-life are now for the first time about to be related.

CHAPTER II

CANONICUS MAKES TROUBLE

The boy thus introduced was carefully trained for the high position that he must some time fill. Although from his father he never heard an impatient or an unkind word, he was taught to respect his elders and to yield the most implicit obedience to those in authority over him. As soon as he was old enough to comprehend what he heard and saw he was permitted to sit beside the Peacemaker and listen to the discussion of matters affecting the well-being of the tribes. From Longfeather himself, from the old men of the village, and from the visitors who journeyed to it Nahma learned the traditions of his people. His father also taught him to distinguish the totems of tribes or clans, together with their significance, and illustrated his lessons by means of the pictured belts that hung in the council-house. From these same teachers Nahma also learned to believe in witchcraft and magic, by which alone were they able to account for many natural phenomena. Thus even in the years of his youth there came to Nahma a wisdom beyond that of all other lads, and his name became known from one end of the land to the other.

Nor during this time of mental training was that of his body neglected. Every day, even in the depth of winter, when ice must be broken before water could be reached, he was made to plunge into the river or the sea to toughen him and harden his flesh. He was taught to swim and to paddle a canoe before he could walk; and often in later years when trained runners were sent by Longfeather with messages to distant tribes, the lad was allowed to accompany them, that he might learn the trails, familiarize himself with remote localities and people, and acquire the art of traversing great spaces in the shortest possible time. So fleet of foot and so strong of wind did he thus become that he at one time covered the distance between the village of Peace and the sand-dunes of the Nausets on the edge of the great salt water between two suns, a feat never before accomplished, and at which all men marvelled.

After this Nahma was frequently chosen to be his father's messenger on occasions of importance, and very proud was the young warrior of the trust thus reposed in him. Thus it happened that one day in the lad's eighteenth year, when a matter of grave import demanded prompt communication with a distant point in a region of danger, Longfeather naturally turned to Nahma, his son.

Troublous times had come, and the safety of the region so long ruled by the Peacemaker was seriously threatened. To consider the situation Longfeather had assembled a council of the tribes at Montaup, on the edge of the salt water. This was the great gathering-place of the Wampanoags, and to it their chieftain with his family was accustomed to resort during the heated months of each summer. So here the council was met, and after the calumet had passed entirely around its seated circle Longfeather addressed the chiefs as follows:

"It is well that we are come together, for the shadow of trouble is upon us like that of a black cloud hiding the sun. While we be of many tribes we have until now been of one heart, and even from the days of Nassaup, my father, have we dwelt at peace one with another. Now, however, is that peace threatened, and I have summoned you to see what may be done."

Here the speaker took one from a bundle of small sticks and handed it to the oldest chief, saying, "Take this peace-stick, my brother, and remember its meaning." Then to the others he continued,—

"For a long time, from our fathers, and from their fathers before them, have we heard tales of strange, white-skinned beings armed with thunderbolts, who have come from the sea. We have listened with trembling, but have comforted ourselves that these strangers, whom we took to be gods, appeared not on our shores, but at places far removed. Also we heard that they tarried not; but always, after a short stay, departed as they had come. Take this stick, my brother, and regard it with respect, for it indicates the belief of our fathers."

Thus saying, Longfeather handed a second stick from his bundle to the aged chief. Then resuming his address, he said,—

"But all our comfort has vanished with the gaining of wisdom. Nearer and more frequent have come tales of the whiteskins, until now we know them to be men like unto ourselves, only of a different color and having hairy faces. They are armed with thunder-sticks that can kill at three times the flight of our strongest arrows. Also have we learned that these men are borne to our coast in mighty canoes built by themselves and driven by the wind. We know that many of these canoes come for fish to the salt waters of the Tarratines. Not only do they thus come and go in ever-increasing numbers, but they even visit the land to care for the fish they have taken. Accept this stick, my brother, to remind thee of the white-skinned men who fish." With this Longfeather handed a third stick to the old man.

"Still," he continued, "the white fish-catchers do not attempt to remain with us, nor have they thus far given us cause to fear them. Some of their lesser canoes, small when compared with those in which they come and go, but large by the side of ours, even as the eagle is larger than the hawk, have drifted empty to our shores, and our young men have made use of them. Also at times the great winged canoes of the white men have been seen to pass our coast, but never until the season of last corn-planting have they tarried. Then came one to the country of the Narragansetts, where it remained for the space of three moons. This stick, my brother, will refresh thy memory concerning the coming and tarrying of the great white canoe." With this the speaker passed a fourth stick to the old chief. Then deliberately and with emphasis he resumed his speech, saying,—

"On an island that they occupied the strangers who came in this canoe erected a lodge. Many of you have seen it and them. They roamed through the forest making thunder and killing beasts with their fire-sticks. Above all, they traded with the Narragansetts, giving them knives and hatchets made of an unknown metal, strong and sharp, kettles that fire may not harm, and many other things in exchange for skins of the beaver. Only with their thunder-sticks they would not part. By many it was feared that they would remain and attempt to possess the land that is our land. But after a time they departed, and the heart of Longfeather was glad when he knew they were gone. At the same moment his heart was again made heavy, for they gave out that they would come again, bringing great wealth to exchange for beaver. Take this stick, my brother, to remind thee that the white men will come again.

"Now, my friends, what has happened? It is this. The Narragansetts are puffed up with pride because they are possessed of knives and hatchets better and more deadly than any ever before seen in all the world. Also, they desire to obtain more of such things and to learn the secret of the thunder-sticks that kill as far as one may see. Therefore did Canonicus, head sachem of the Narragansetts, propose secretly to me that when the great canoe came again I should order the white men to be killed, that he and I might possess ourselves of their wealth, and so become as gods, all-powerful in the land. This stick, my brother, marks the proposition of Canonicus.

"To the evil words of the Narragansett I refused to listen, saying to him that to do what he had in his mind would surely bring upon our heads the wrath of the Great Spirit. Furthermore, I bade Canonicus put such evil thoughts far behind him and consider them no more. This stick, my brother, is Longfeather's answer to Canonicus.

"Again, my friends, what has happened? The Narragansett promised to open wide his ears that the words of Longfeather might sink into his heart. Did he do this? No. He closed tight his ears that they might not hear, and began to look for others who would aid him in his wickedness. So far did his eyes travel that they came even to the land of the Maquas [Mohawks], who from the days of the first men have been our enemies. To them is he preparing to send messengers with presents and a promise of great wealth, together with power over all the tribes, if they will join him in destroying the next white men who may come. Canonicus was bidden to this council, but I cannot see him. This stick, my brother, will tell thee of his black heart. I have finished."

So long did the council discuss this situation and so many were the speeches to be delivered on the subject, that a decision was not reached until late on the second day of meeting. Then it was ordered that Canonicus should be summoned to report in person to the assembled chiefs, who for two days longer would await his coming. If at the end of that time he had not appeared, a war-party of the allied tribes should be sent to fetch him. In the mean time Longfeather would send a delegation to the Maquas bearing presents, and offering, on behalf of the combined New England tribes, a treaty that should secure to all equal benefits from whatever trade might be had with the white-skinned strangers. It was furthermore agreed that so long as the white men proved themselves friendly they should be treated as friends. "For," said the Peacemaker, "they are few and we are many, they are weak while we are strong, therefore let us live at peace with them, if indeed they come to us again, a thing that I trust may not happen. So shall we please the Great Spirit who made them, doubtless for some good reason, even as he made the red man and gave him control over the earth."

So it was done even as the council had ordered, and a runner was despatched to Canonicus with a summons for him to appear at Montaup, and forbidding him to treat with the Maquas. Also active preparations were made for sending an embassy to that powerful people on behalf of the allied New England tribes, and to his joy Nahma was chosen to accompany it as his father's representative.

CHAPTER III

AT THE CROSSING OF THE SHATEMUC

The whole land to the very edge of the great salt water, and including the islands of the sea, was covered with a forest that sheltered it alike from summer heats and the deadly cold of winter. Stately pines growing on hill-sides lifted their evergreen heads far above all other trees, and stood as ever-watchful sentinels. Mighty oaks shaded wide-spread areas, while graceful elms were mirrored in lake and river. Everywhere the painted maples flaunted their brilliant colors, while chestnut, beech, hickory, and walnut showered down bountiful stores of food to those trusting in them for a winter's supply. Man, beast, and bird, all children of the forest, dwelt within its safe protection and were fed from its exhaustless abundance. Its rivers and smaller streams, filled from brimming reservoirs and unobstructed by dams, afforded highways of travel ever ready for use and always in the best of repair. Besides these, the forest was threaded with trails worn by countless generations of Indian runners, traders, hunters, and fighters, and these were as familiar to the dwellers in the shade as are the streets of a city to one born within its walls.

Along one of these devious trails, narrow and so dim that an unpractised eye would quickly have lost it, sped a solitary runner. He was young and goodly to look upon, while his movements were as graceful as those of the deer, whose soft-tanned skins constituted his attire. He was bareheaded, and in his hair was fastened a single feather from the wing of an osprey or fishing eagle.

A noticeable feature of his costume was a broad belt of wampum, worn diagonally across his breast so that it might readily be seen and recognized. On it at short intervals were worked seven figures representing birds, beasts, and fishes, for it was the Belt of Seven Totems, indicating the authority of Longfeather the Peacemaker, and the young runner now wearing it so conspicuously was none other than Nahma, his only son.

While Longfeather awaited the return of his messenger to Canonicus and made ready the presents intended for Sacandaga, chief sachem of the Maquas, news came that the Narragansett embassy to that same powerful chieftain had already set forth on its mission. Thus there was no time to be lost if his own message was to reach Sacandaga first, an event that he deemed to be of the utmost importance. The chiefs whom he desired to send as ambassadors could not travel at greater speed than could the Narragansetts, who had a two days' start, but it was possible that a fleet-footed runner might even yet overtake and pass them. As this thought flashed through Longfeather's mind he knew that if the thing might be done it could only be accomplished by the swiftest of all his runners, and he promptly caused Nahma to be summoned.

At that moment the young warrior was listening with eager interest to the stories of white men and their great winged canoes, told by Samoset, an Abenaki youth of his own age, who had accompanied his chieftain to the council at Montaup.

"What do they call their tribe?" inquired Nahma, "and of what nature is their speech? Doth it resemble ours so that one may comprehend their words?"

"They appear to be of many tribes," replied Samoset, "though we call them all 'Yengeese.' Also they speak with many tongues, strange and unpleasant to the ear."

"What are they like, these tongues? Hast thou not caught some word that we may hear?"

"Often they say 'Hillo' and 'Sacré,'" replied Samoset, "but what these mean I know not. Also, once, where from hiding I watched them cooking fish on a beach, a pebble rolled from me to them. As they sprang up in alarm I slipped away, fearing lest they might take offence. As I did so one of them cried out very loud, 'Mass i-sawit!'" (By the mass I saw it.)

"Massasoit," repeated Nahma, thoughtfully. "It hath a familiar sound, and might be a word of the Wampanoags, except that it is without meaning. I long greatly to see these white-skinned fish-catchers and their big canoes that resemble floating hill-tops with trees growing in them. So if it may be arranged I will return with thee, Samoset, to look upon these wonders. But you have said naught of the thunder-sticks about which we hear so much. What of them? Are they indeed as terrible as represented?"

Ere Samoset could answer, Nahma received word that Longfeather desired his presence, and, promising shortly to rejoin his companions, he left them. Ten minutes later, without their knowledge or that of any person in all Montaup, save only his parents, the young runner had left his father's lodge bound on a solitary mission, longer, more important, and more dangerous than any he had heretofore undertaken. He was to make his way with all speed and in utmost secrecy to Sacandaga, head sachem of the Maquas, and urge him, in the name of Longfeather, not to treat with the Narragansetts or any other single tribe before the arrival of the Peacemaker's own embassy.

Longfeather had given his instructions hastily and in a few words. He had invested the lad with his own superb belt as a badge of authority, and had dismissed him with the peremptory orders of a sachem, delivered in the loving tone of a father who sends his only son into danger.

Besides the Belt of Seven Totems, Nahma carried only a bow and arrows slung to his back, a wallet of parched corn bruised in a mortar until it formed a coarse meal, a small fire-bag of flints and tinder, and a copper knife, the precious gift of his father. Having taken but five minutes for preparation, he tenderly embraced his mother and bade her farewell. Filled with a presentiment of coming evil, Miantomet clung to him as though she could not let him go; but, comforting her with loving words, the lad gently disengaged her arms from about his neck and sprang away. In another minute he had plunged into the forest and was lost to sight amid its blackness.

For some hours the way was partially revealed by the light of a young moon, and by the time of its setting Nahma had placed a score of miles between him and Montaup. Then, as he could no longer make speed through the darkness, he flung himself down at the foot of a great oak and was almost instantly fast asleep.

By earliest dawn he was again on the trail, and all that day he sped forward with hardly a pause. Occasionally he passed a group of bark huts nestled beside some smooth-flowing stream and surrounded by rudely tilled fields; but at none of these did he halt, save only now and then for a few mouthfuls of food. The belt that he wore insured him everywhere a glad welcome and instant service. He forded or swam the smaller streams; while at points where his trail crossed rivers he always found canoes that he did not hesitate to appropriate to his own use if their owners were not at hand. He was on the king's business and nothing might delay it.

Thus Nahma sped so swiftly on his errand that an hour before sunset of the second day found him, very weary but exultant, on the eastern bank of the Shatemuc and at the border of the country claimed by the Iroquois, of whom the Maquas were the easternmost tribe. He was farther from home than he had ever been before and in a region of which he had no knowledge. At the same time he knew that the Maquas, being now at peace with the New England tribes, were accustomed to send hunting-parties east of their great river, and so he had hoped to find one or more canoes at the crossing. In this, however, he was disappointed, for, search as he might, he could discover none of the desired craft, though he found a place where several had but recently been concealed.

As there were no other traces of human presence in that vicinity, Nahma concluded that the canoes had been taken by persons coming from across the river. He did not suspect that it might have been done by the Narragansetts whom he was striving to outstrip; for thus far he had discovered no sign of them, and had reached a conclusion that they must have taken some other trail. At any rate, there was no canoe to be had, and, as he was determined to cross the river before dark, he must swim it. This he did, keeping dry his scanty clothing and few belongings by floating them on a small raft of bark that he pushed before him. Arrived on the farther side our young runner made a startling discovery. Not only were a number of canoes drawn out on the bank and concealed beneath overhanging bushes, but on the soft ground beside them he found the unmistakable imprint of Narragansett moccasins. Also, a short distance back from the river, he came upon the still smouldering remains of a small fire. At length, then, he was close upon the heels of his rivals, and he must at all hazards pass them that night in order to gain a first hearing from Sacandaga. At the same time he was in immediate need of food and rest, for he was faint with hunger and exhausted by his recent exertions. There was no sign of danger, his rivals had gone on, and the fire they had so kindly provided invited him to cook food that was to be had for the taking.

So abounding with fish were all the streams of that land that no one possessed of even ordinary skill at catching them need go hungry. Nahma was well aware of this, and, taking a pinch of his parched corn, he stepped back to the river's bank and cast it upon the water. In another moment he had transfixed with an unerring arrow one of the half-dozen large fish that rushed greedily to the surface, and his supper was provided. Having cooked it and satisfied his ravenous hunger, the lad withdrew to a thicket well beyond the circle of firelight and flung himself down for an hour of sleep before continuing his journey.

The young runner was lost to consciousness within a minute after closing his eyes; but not until his heavy breathing gave notice of the fact did a painted savage, who for more than an hour had watched his every movement, drop to the ground from among the branches of a thick-leaved oak. There he had crouched as motionless as a panther awaiting its prey; and now, after stretching his cramped limbs, he stole with catlike tread towards the sleeping youth.

CHAPTER IV

THE BELT CHANGES HANDS

In all the history of the world it has happened that dwellers by the sea have been more advanced and prosperous than their inland neighbors. Thus, in the present instance, the Wampanoags and the Narragansetts were the most numerous and powerful of the New England tribes. There had always been jealousies and often open warfare between them, nor had these wholly ceased to exist upon the election of Longfeather to the high office of Peacemaker. Canonicus, head sachem of the Narragansetts, felt that he was equally entitled to be thus honored, and consequently was bitterly jealous of his successful rival. This feeling was shared by his nephew and adopted son, Miantinomo, only that the envy and hatred of the latter were directed against Nahma, whose place as future ruler of the allied tribes he was determined to occupy, if by any means such a thing might be accomplished.

Thus, when Canonicus planned to secure a power greater than that of Longfeather by forming an alliance with the eastern Iroquois, he found in Miantinomo an eager assistant. So, even as the Peacemaker had chosen his own son to represent him in the mission to Sacandaga, Canonicus selected Miantinomo for a similar position in the Narragansett embassy. In this way, without either being aware of the fact, the two young rivals became actively pitted against each other in the most important undertaking of their lives.

While urged to make all possible haste, the Narragansett party was obliged to adapt its pace to that of the oldest chief among them; and while they expected that Longfeather would also send messengers to the Maquas, they fancied these would be equally restricted as to speed. They knew that they had a start of at least two days, and believed they could reach Sacandaga's village, transact their business, and depart for home before the coming of their rivals. At the same time they neglected no precaution to insure the success of their undertaking. They struck the Shatemuc at a point much lower than that reached by Nahma, and from it ascended the river in canoes. As they advanced they kept sharp watch of the eastern shore, and removed all craft found on it to the opposite side of the river. Their last exploit of this kind was at a place where they must again take to the land and follow a trail to the Maqua villages.

Having thus provided for a further delay of the other party, they felt no apprehension of being overtaken, and proceeded leisurely on their journey. They did, however, take the added precaution of leaving a scout behind them to watch the crossing until sunset. For this purpose they selected Miantinomo, as being the keenest-eyed and swiftest-footed of their party. So Nahma's most active rival and secret enemy was left to cover the rear, while his elders disappeared in single file up the narrow trail.

According to Indian custom Miantinomo had brought pigments with him, and now he relieved the tedium of his watch, which he did not believe would amount to anything, by painting his body in anticipation of a speedy arrival at the Maqua villages. So interested was he in this occupation that for a time he forgot everything else; then, startled by a splash in the river, he glanced up. A swimmer, just emerged from deep water, was wading ashore pushing before him a small raft, and Miantinomo instantly recognized him. Being hidden behind a screen of bushes, and satisfied that Nahma was still ignorant of his presence, the young Narragansett, crouching low, made his way to a thick-leaved oak that overhung the trail a short distance back from the river, and was snugly hidden among its branches by the time Nahma gained the land.

Miantinomo was not wholly surprised to discover the son of Longfeather at this place; but he could not understand why he should be alone. It must be that he had come to obtain canoes in which to bring over the others of his party. Thus thinking, he expected to see Nahma at once recross the river. In that case he would hasten after his own companions and urge them to travel all night, that they might still reach the Maqua villages in advance of their rivals.

But the new-comer failed to do as expected, and Miantinomo was more puzzled than ever at witnessing his preparations to secure a meal and spend some time where he was. He evidently was alone, and after the spy became convinced of this, he wondered if by some means he might not prevent Longfeather's messenger from continuing his journey. He was also filled with a great longing to possess himself of the Belt of Seven Totems, which he recognized as Nahma again assumed it. Well did the young Narragansett realize the power conferred upon the wearer of that belt. If it should be opposed to him in the presence of Sacandaga, then would his mission prove a failure and his uncle's cherished plan would come to naught. On the other hand, if the all-powerful belt could be made to appear in his behalf, if he only might possess it even for a short time, how easy would become his task!

From the moment these thoughts entered his mind Miantinomo was determined to acquire the coveted object by any means that should offer. He knew that Nahma would never relinquish the belt of his own free will, and that it must be taken from him by either stealth or force. He knew also that should he succeed in his wicked design he would incur the vengeance of Longfeather, and doubtless bring on a war in which all the New England tribes would be involved. But what of that? Would not the powerful Iroquois fight on the side of the Narragansetts; and, armed with the white man's weapons, might they not successfully defy the world?

Filled with these ambitious thoughts, Miantinomo flattened himself closer against the great oak limb and, regardless of the discomfort of his position, watched with glittering eyes every movement of his rival. More than anything else he resembled a venomous serpent awaiting an opportunity to spring upon an unsuspecting victim. At his back was a bow and a quiver of flint-headed arrows, with one of which he might easily have stricken Nahma to the earth at any moment, but he was not yet prepared to shed innocent blood for the accomplishment of his purpose. Besides, he dared not make a movement that might attract the other's attention. So he waited with all the patience of his race and an ever-strengthening resolve to obtain possession of the Peacemaker's belt.

In the mean time Nahma, utterly unconscious of the dangerous presence so close at hand, procured, cooked, and ate his supper, selected what he believed to be a safe resting-place, and laid himself down for a nap. The moment for which Miantinomo had waited was at hand, and with noiseless movement he slipped to the ground. For a few seconds he stood motionless behind the tree, to assure himself that his rival had not been aroused; then with catlike tread he stole towards the unsuspecting sleeper.

At length he stood beside Nahma and bent over him with the coveted belt easily within his reach. Bits of moonlight sifting through leafy branches fell upon it and upon the upturned face of the sleeper. So profound was his slumber that Miantinomo believed he might remove the belt without disturbing him, and laying his stone-headed war-club within easy reach, he began with the utmost caution to make the attempt. It had very nearly succeeded, and the belt, partially loosened, was within his grasp, when, without warning, Nahma opened his eyes. Miantinomo leaped back at the first sign of waking, and as his victim attempted to gain his feet a crushing blow stretched him again on the ground motionless and to all appearance dead.

For a moment the young Narragansett stood ready to repeat his cowardly assault; but, seeing that a second blow was unnecessary, he again bent over the body of his rival and snatched from it the belt for which he had been willing to risk so much. With his prize thus secured, he was about to hasten from the spot when another thought caused him to pause. It would never do to leave the evidence of his crime where it was so certain to be discovered. He had not meant to kill Nahma, and now that the awful deed was committed, he trembled at thought of its possible consequences. Even his own people would regard him with abhorrence if they knew of it, while the vengeance of

Longfeather would be swift and terrible. Therefore what he had done must never be known even by his nearest friends, and before leaving that spot he must remove all traces of his murderous deed. Stripping off his scanty raiment that it might not become bloodstained, he lifted the limp form of the stricken youth, and carrying it some distance down the stream, flung it into the river. He heard the heavy splash of the body as it struck the water, but was too nervous to make further inquiry as to its condition. Thus whether it sank or floated he did not know, nor did he seek to discover, but fled from the spot as though pursued.

Reaching the place where he had left his garments and the belt, he hastily resumed the former, and concealed the latter beneath them. Then he set forth at top speed to rejoin his companions and report that he had seen nothing alarming during his watch by the river-side.

On the following day the Narragansett embassy reached the Maqua villages, where, in spite of their alluring proposition and valuable presents, they were at first received with coldness and suspicion. At the council assembled to hear their talk Sacandaga flatly refused to make an alliance with any one of the New England tribes, and the Narragansetts retired from it believing that the cherished plan of Canonicus must come to naught.

That night, however, Miantinomo sought a private interview with the Maqua sachem, and displayed to him the Belt of Seven Totems, which Sacandaga at once recognized, since its fame had spread far and wide. "It is the belt of Longfeather," he said, after a close inspection.

"Yes," replied Miantinomo, "it is the belt of the great Peacemaker, who is also my father."

"How can that be?" asked the other. "May a man have two fathers?"

"By adoption, yes," answered the young Narragansett. "Having no son of his own, Longfeather has adopted the nephew of his friend Canonicus, that in time their tribes may be united under one chief. To the Narragansetts I am known as Miantinomo, but by all others am I called Nahma, son of Longfeather."

"I have heard the name and it is described as being that of a most promising warrior," said Sacandaga, regarding the young man with renewed interest.

"One blessed with two such fathers should indeed prove himself worthy," was the modest reply. "In proof that I am regarded as a son by Longfeather," he continued, "the Peacemaker has intrusted me with this token of authority. Never before has he parted with it, and to none, save only the mighty chief of the Maquas, whose friendship he greatly desires, would he send it. Also he has done this thing in secret, so that even those who come with me know not that I am intrusted with so great authority."

So impressed was Sacandaga by this flattering statement and by sight of the belt offered in evidence of its sincerity, that he not only listened attentively to the young man's proposals, but finally agreed to accept them.

"With Canonicus alone I could not have treated," he said, "for he is but one of many; but with Longfeather, who represents the many, I may enter into a compact."

"The words of Sacandaga are good," replied Miantinomo, gravely, "and will be as the singing of birds in the ears of Longfeather. At the same time I trust it will not be forgotten that they may not be sent directly to him. For the present he would not have it known that he desires the wealth of the white-skinned strangers. If they think him a friend they will the more readily fall into the snare he will set for them. Therefore, my father, let the public treaty be made only between Sacandaga and Canonicus, for Longfeather will be well pleased to have it so proclaimed."

"I understand and will not forget," replied the Maqua chief.

Thus through treachery and deceit did the wily young Narragansett gain his point and accomplish the mission with which he had been intrusted by Canonicus.

CHAPTER V

WHAT THE DAUGHTERS
OF KAWERAS FOUND

Sacandaga secretly gave to Miantinomo a belt of wampum bearing the emblem of a tortoise, his own totem, to be transmitted to Longfeather, while publicly he gave another to the Narragansett chiefs for Canonicus. After the formalities of the treaty as well as the private negotiations were concluded, Miantinomo urged the immediate departure of his companions lest they might discover his evil doings. Then, having got them well started on their homeward journey, he hastened on in advance. For this he gave an excuse that the whites who were to be plundered might appear at any time, and that every hour was now of importance. His real reason was the belief that Longfeather must also have sent a delegation of chiefs to confer with the Maquas, and a determination to meet them and, if possible, turn them back. So, while his companions took a trail different from the one by which they had come, Miantinomo hastened back to the place where he had encountered Nahma, and found those who had followed the son of Longfeather camped on the opposite bank of the river awaiting the coming of canoes in which to cross over.

For some time after his appearance among them they asked no questions, but waited in dignified silence to learn of his errand to them. Finally, the young man said,—

"My fathers, you are following Nahma, the son of Longfeather, on a mission to Sacandaga, the Iroquois. Is it not so?"

"It is as my young brother has said," replied one of the chiefs.

"Then you may be spared a farther journey," continued Miantinomo, "for Nahma, by virtue of the belt he wore, the great Belt of Seven Totems, readily gained the ear of Sacandaga, even while I and those with me were vainly striving to do so. Thus did he make a treaty with the Iroquois on behalf of Longfeather, his father, and for fear that you might claim a share in the honor he has returned to Montaup by another trail. Even now he travels with those of my people who kept me company. I have come by this trail that I may visit the village of Peace before returning to my father. For this I was heavy-hearted; but now am I glad, because I have met with you, and may so save you a useless journey."

For some time the chiefs discussed this report of Miantinomo; and then, because they did not wholly trust him, they decided to retain him as a hostage while one of their number visited the Maqua villages for confirmation of his words.

During the absence of this messenger Miantinomo was filled with apprehension, though he carefully hid his feelings and affected the utmost unconcern. He even went so far as to advise Longfeather's commissioners to appropriate to their own use the presents they were bearing to Sacandaga, and seek their respective homes without reporting to the Peacemaker.

"The treaty has been made," he said. "The sachem of the Maquas is satisfied and expects nothing further. You have been put to much trouble and will have no share in the honor. Longfeather has no thought that the presents will be returned to him. Therefore is it best that you who have earned them should keep them."

To such arguments the chiefs listened not unwillingly; and when their messenger returned with a report that Miantinomo had spoken truly concerning what had taken place in the Maqua village, they decided to accept his advice.

"Why should Longfeather have intrusted the Belt of Seven Totems to one so young and inexperienced as Nahma instead of to us?" they asked. "Also why did he not tell us that he had done so? Truly he has shamed us, and if we take his presents to wipe out our shame, then shall we do that which is right and good."

Having reached this conclusion, each took a share and went his way; while Miantinomo, rejoicing at the complete success of his evil designs and still wearing next his skin the Belt of Seven Totems that was the badge of highest authority in all that land, returned to his own people. There he busied himself with the secret spreading of various reports concerning the young rival with whom he had dealt so foully. One was that Nahma had taken a Maqua girl to wife and would thereafter dwell among the Iroquois. Another was to the effect that he had been murdered by his companions of Longfeather's embassy for the sake of the belt that he wore, as well as for the presents intrusted to them, which they had taken for their own benefit.

From Sacandaga himself Longfeather learned that a young man named Nahma and wearing the Belt of Seven Totems had indeed visited the Maqua villages, from which he had departed again in company with the Narragansett chiefs. Although the latter denied this and declared that they had not seen Nahma, Miantinomo maintained that he had met him in Sacandaga's village and spoken with him.

By these and other conflicting stories was the fate of Nahma so shrouded in mystery that it became impossible to discover what had really befallen him, and finally his friends mourned for him as for one who is dead. Even while they thus mourned it became rumored that either Canonicus or Mian-tinomo, his adopted son, would succeed Longfeather in the high office of Peacemaker and ruler of the allied New England tribes.

In the mean time, while all these events were happening, Nahma knew nothing of them nor indeed of anything else, for he lay tossing with fever in the lodge of Kaweras, principal arrow-maker of the Maquas. When, apparently dead, he had been flung into the river to disappear forever from human eyes, he had fallen among a bed of reeds in a place where the water was too shallow to drown him. There he lay motionless through the long night hours, half in the water and half out of it, while the tall reeds whispered and rustled above his head. Soft-flitting night-birds gazed at him with wondering eyes, while timid animals coming to the river to drink sniffed the air tainted by his presence and fled in terror.

Towards morning a glimmer of returning life entered the numbed brain, and in striving to obey its commands the poor bruised body began to make feeble movements. By sunrise Nahma was sitting up and gazing stupidly at the green wall by which he was surrounded. Also he muttered over and over, with tedious repetition, three meaningless words: "Hillo, Sacré," and "Massasoit." Other than this he gave no sign of restored consciousness. He did not take heed even when a sound of merry voices came to the place where he sat, nor was his attention attracted by a loud swish and rustle of the reeds that came ever nearer until it was close at hand. Then there was a momentary silence, broken only by the monotonous repetition of "Hillo, Sacré, Massasoit."

A stifled exclamation and excited whispers announced that these words had at length reached human ears, but there was an evident hesitation while fear struggled with curiosity. After a minute the reeds in front of Nahma were noiselessly parted, and the bow of a canoe stole into sight inch by inch with almost imperceptible motion. From it peered the face of a young girl, bright and fascinating, but big-eyed with apprehension as that of a startled fawn. As she caught a glimpse of the wounded youth the progress of the canoe was instantly arrested, while the girl became rigidly motionless. Her eyes, however, took in every detail of his appearance and of his melancholy situation. He still appeared to see nothing and still repeated the words that had attracted attention, "Hillo, Sacré, Massasoit."

"What is it, sister? What do you see?" came in a frightened whisper from an unseen speaker who occupied the farther end of the canoe; but the other, still gazing motionless, made no reply. "Aeana," insisted the invisible one in a louder tone, "tell me quickly what you see. I am frightened."

"I see nothing to be afraid of, Otshata," replied the girl in the bow of the canoe. "It is a young man, but he is evidently sorely wounded and regards not our presence. There, you may see for yourself." With this the girl called Aeana pulled the canoe into such a position that the other could catch a glimpse of Nahma.

"It is certain that he is handsome," whispered Otshata; "but is not his condition dreadful? Let us hasten and report it to our father."

"No," answered Aeana, decisively. "That is," she added, "we will return to our father, and that quickly, but we must either take this young man with us or leave him to perish. See you not that the river is flowing backward and that its waters are rising? If we leave him he must die, since he is in no condition to care for himself. How we may get him into the canoe I know not, but if that can be done we will carry him to Kaweras, our father."

The elder though more timid sister attempted a further expostulation, but without heeding her Aeana brought the canoe close to where the wounded youth still sat, indifferent alike to his fate and his surroundings, idly repeating the strange words that had fixed themselves in his bewildered brain. Aeana spoke to him, but he failed to comprehend what she said. She laid a gentle hand on his arm and endeavored to persuade him into the canoe, but he sat passively motionless.

Finally in despair the girl uttered one of the strange words that he so constantly repeated. "Massasoit," she said, and the youth looked at her, seeming for the first time to recognize her presence. A faint smile flickered across his blood-smeared features, and he made a movement towards her. In another moment, aided by her supple strength, he had gained the interior of the canoe, and lay weakly with closed eyes while the two girls pulled it out from among the reeds. Then seizing their paddles, they urged the light craft swiftly down the river towards their father's lodge.

Thus did the daughters of Kaweras, who had been sent to fetch a bundle of stout reeds that might serve as shafts for bird arrows, return without them, but bringing a wounded and unconscious youth in their place.

Although the old arrow-maker saw at a glance that the young warrior was not of the Maqua, nor even of the Iroquois people, his ideas of hospitality did not permit him to ask questions nor hesitate a moment before attending to the stranger's needs. It required the united strength of father and daughters to transfer Nahma from canoe to lodge, and when he was finally laid in the latter on a hastily improvised couch of boughs and skins, he was once more to all appearance dead.

CHAPTER VI

IN THE LODGE OF THE ARROW-MAKER

The lodge of Kaweras, occupied only by him and his two daughters, stood by itself in a grassy glade shaded by elms on the western bank of the lordly Shatemuc. Close at hand flowed a spring of crystal water, while at no great distances were abundant materials for the prosecution of the old arrow-maker's trade. Nearby hills furnished him with flints and slate, agate and milk-white quartz; stout reeds and tough, straight-grained woods were to be had for the taking. Deer of the forest yielded him their strong back-sinews for binding arrow-head to shaft, and myriads of sea-fowl flying up or down the broad river gave him of their feathers. In his younger days Kaweras had been a noted warrior. Now he was the most expert arrow-maker of the region in which he dwelt. He was also a mystic, a prophet, and one well versed in the science of healing by means of herbs, roots, bark, and leaves.

In his double capacity of arrow-maker and medicine-man Kaweras was much sought after, and though his lodge stood remote from any village of his people, it was rarely without visitors. Young warriors came for arrows and to catch glimpses of his pretty daughters; their elders came to consult with him concerning grave affairs; while many of all ages and both sexes came for healing or to profit by his advice. As all brought gifts, Kaweras was well-to-do, and his larder was always stocked with choicest products of forest and field without effort on his own part or that of his daughters.

These last kept tidy the spacious lodge with its three divisions, of which only the outer one was for the general public, prepared the family meals, and did much sewing with needles of fishbone threaded with fibre or sinew. At the same time they found abundant leisure for paddling on the river in their canoe of white birch brought from the far north and for attending to the needs of their pets, two tame fawns and a large flock of wild ducks bred in captivity. Also they helped their father in the making of arrows, and especially in the gathering of material.

With this busy but uneventful life the elder sister was quite content, but Aeana always longed for excitement and adventure. Now she had found both in the coming to their quiet lodge of a stranger, young, mysterious, wounded to the point of death, and speaking a language to which even the wisdom of her father could find no clue. Furthermore, she regarded him with a proprietary interest, for had she not discovered him and rescued him from almost certain destruction?

During the long illness that followed his coming, and while he lay oblivious to his surroundings, she often gazed curiously upon his face, listened to the three strange words that he repeated to the exclusion of all others, and speculated concerning him. She became impatient for him to get well that he might tell her who he was, where he came from, and how he happened to be in the sad plight that had so nearly proved fatal. She would have talked of him to their many visitors but for her father's expressed wish that Nahma's presence in their lodge should be kept a secret from all men. Kaweras hoped thus to learn something concerning him from unguarded conversations, but in this he was disappointed. It is true that he heard of the mysterious disappearance of Nahma, the son of Longfeather, but whenever that youth was mentioned Miantinomo was described, and as this description did not coincide in any particular with the appearance of his patient, he had no reason to connect the two.

Otshata was quite as much interested in the young stranger as was her sister, but in another way. She thought him very handsome, which Aeana would not admit, and secretly rejoiced in the helplessness that depended so largely upon her gentle ministrations. She had the motherly instinct that found pleasure in self-sacrifice, and from the first constituted herself chief nurse of the stricken youth.

For a long time it was doubtful if Nahma would ever recover from the illness by which he was prostrated; but after it finally took a turn for the better he began rapidly to mend. On the day that he first ventured outside the lodge into the freedom of open air there was much rejoicing in the little family, but it was tinged with sadness. Although weak and emaciated from his long sickness, he was still a goodly youth to look upon, and gave promise of speedily regaining his physical powers; but his mind was that of a child. He could neither tell nor remember anything of his former life, even its language was lost to him, and he could converse only in such words of the Iroquois tongue as he had acquired from his present associates. As he could not tell them his name, they called him "Massasoit," from the word he had most frequently uttered during his delirium, and this he accepted as readily as he did all else that they offered him.

While thus compelled to relearn everything that required mental effort, it was soon discovered that he had lost none of his cunning in matters calling for physical strength or skill. He could still shoot an arrow or hurl a spear with unerring aim, was rarely at fault on the dimmest trail, and proved himself an adept in such branches of Indian handiwork as usually fell to the share of warriors, such as the fashioning of weapons or the building of canoes. He soon regained a muscular strength even greater than that with which he had been endowed before his illness, while his fleetness of foot excited the wonder of his friends.

With all this Nahma was gentle and submissive to authority, a trait that aroused the utmost scorn in the mind of Aeana. From the time his mental weakness was discovered this high-spirited girl treated him as she would a child, bidding him come or go, fetch or carry, according as she felt inclined, and apparently she despised him for his ready obedience to her orders. He, on the other hand, regarded her with an intense admiration and sought in every way to win her favor. All his trophies of the chase were laid at her feet only to be contemptuously rejected or flung to Otshata. In the latter, however, the young man found a friend to whom his misfortune appealed so keenly that she treated him with unwearied kindness and tenderest consideration. He called her "sister," a term that he dared not apply to Aeana, and poured all his troubles into her sympathetic ear.

One day Nahma returned hot and weary from a chase that had lasted many hours and presented a noble stag to Aeana. Without taking notice of the gift, and careless of his evident weariness, she bade him fetch her water from the spring. As he willingly departed on this mission she regarded him with curling lip, and when he returned bearing a large earthen jar of water that he set before her, she promptly overturned it so that its contents were spilled. At the same time she uttered the single word "squaw" with an accent of utter contempt and entered the lodge, leaving him bewildered and mortified.

Walking slowly towards the river, he discovered Otshata seated in a shaded nook on its bank embroidering a moccasin with painted quills.

"My sister, why does Aeana hate me?" he asked, as he flung himself despondently on the turf beside her.

"She hates thee not, my brother," replied the other, interrupting her work to look at him.

"Truly she does. In every word and by every act she shows her dislike," declared Nahma, bitterly. "She would be glad never to see me more, and I will go away rather than remain longer to displease her by my presence."

"Speak not of such a thing!" exclaimed Otshata. "Whither would you go, and what should we do without our hunter? If Aeana seems to treat thee unkindly, it is only to inspire thee with a braver spirit. She likes it not that one come to the estate of a warrior should tamely serve her. She would have thee do brave deeds, and also she would have thee remember thy past. Canst thou not do this, and by hard thinking recall some one thing? Who was thy father? Who struck the cruel blow that so nearly ended thy life? Who are thy people? Are they the Saganaga of the south, the Oneidas of the west, or wast thou born among the fish-eaters who dwell in the country of sunrising? I will not ask if thou hast Huron blood in thy veins; for in spite of thy moccasins I feel assured that thou art not of that wicked people."

By this reference Otshata recalled the fact that, when found wounded in the river sedge, Nahma had on his feet a pair of Huron-made moccasins procured in the village of Peace to replace others worn out by his journey; but of these he could give no account.

"I strive to remember," declared the youth, vehemently. "Night and day, sleeping and waking, I think till my head seems like to burst, but 'tis of no use. The only life that I know is here, and if I have had another, it is gone from me like a dream of the black hours. So it is well that I should go away, and if these Hurons be thy enemies and the enemies of Aeana, then will I go and fight against them that she may no longer despise and hate me."

"No, no!" cried Otshata. "Think not of the war-path, my brother. The Hurons are very fierce and terrible and cruel. Also they are so filled with evil designs that only the wisest and most experienced warriors may hope for success against them. Thee they would easily kill; or, what is worse, they would take advantage of thy simplicity to adopt thee and make thee sharer of their wickedness."

At this point the conversation was interrupted by a summons from Kaweras bidding Massasoit come to him quickly.

While it had been comparatively easy to keep secret the presence of a stranger in the lodge of Kaweras during his illness, it became impossible to do so after he was out and about. So a knowledge of the mysterious youth who could remember nothing of his past speedily became noised abroad, and many persons, attracted by curiosity, came to see him. The victim of these interviews dreaded them so intensely that he spent much time in remote forest depths to avoid them. Now, however, he was fairly caught, and going reluctantly to the lodge, followed at a distance by Otshata, he found himself in the presence of a distinguished-looking chieftain who was seated on a robe beside Kaweras. Behind them stood a group of warriors. As Nahma drew near the eyes of all these were fixed intently upon him, though no word was spoken until he paused within a few paces of his host.

CHAPTER VII

NAHMA JOINS A WAR-PARTY

"Massasoit," said Kaweras, as the young man regarded him inquiringly, "I would have plumes from Ke-neu, the great eagle, to make a war-bonnet. He waits yonder for an invitation to come to us. Can you persuade him?"

With this the speaker pointed upward to where a golden eagle, attracted by a bait of raw flesh placed temptingly at some distance from the lodge, circled on motionless pinions.

Glancing in the direction indicated, Nahma stepped within the lodge, from which he quickly reappeared bearing a bow and three arrows. Again taking his station in front of Kaweras, he stood for a moment motionless, watching intently the movements of the eagle, that still circled slowly downward. One arrow was fitted to the bowstring, while the other two were stuck in the ground before him. Suddenly the youth lifted his weapon and let fly its feathered dart. Then he shot twice more with such marvellous rapidity of motion that the third arrow was leaving the bow ere the first had reached its mark. As the spectators uttered an involuntary exclamation of amazement, the great bird, evidently stricken to its death, plunged dizzily downward with feebly beating wings.

"Bring it," said the sachem, addressing those who stood behind him, and each taking the command to himself, all sprang away in a breathless race for the trophy.

"Do thou bring it," said Kaweras to Nahma.

Instantly the young bowman darted forward with such amazing swiftness that, despite the distance already gained by the others, he overtook and passed them ere they could reach the coveted goal. As he picked up the dead bird and bore it back the others made way for him, nor did one offer to take from him the prize that he had thus twice won. As he laid it at the feet of Kaweras the bird was seen to be transfixed by three arrows.

"The young man should be named Sharp-eye, Quick-hand, and Swift-foot," exclaimed the visiting sachem, who was none other than Sacandaga, "for he has proved himself to excel the best of my warriors in all these things. Not until this day have I believed the tales told me touching his skill; but now I know them to have been less than the truth. If he be as fearless as he is quick he should take high rank as a warrior. How say you, Massasoit? Will you go with me and my young men to do battle with the Hurons, who are reported to have taken the war-path against us?"

For a moment the youth hesitated. He glanced at the old arrow-maker, whose features were unmoved and who made no sign. Then he looked towards Otshata, whose face showed her distress and who made an imploring gesture for him to decline the offer. Finally he turned to Aeana, who stood motionless and with averted gaze, but her attitude and expression were unmistakable. They said as plainly as words, "He is a squaw and dares not face the war-path."

In an instant Nahma's resolution was taken, and he answered Sacandaga, saying,—

"I am without experience of the war-path, nor have I knowledge of any people save only of these, my father and my sisters. If, however, these Hurons be the enemies of Kaweras and of his daughters, then will I gladly go with thee to fight against them."

"It is well," replied Sacandaga, greatly pleased to have gained so promising a recruit. "Spend thou the night with my young men, who will instruct thee concerning many things, and in the morning will we set forth."

Some hours later, when the camp-fires had burned low and the recumbent forms gathered about them were buried in slumber, two men issued silently from the lodge of Kaweras and made their way to a secluded spot on the river-bank, where they believed they might discuss weighty matters without danger of being overheard. They were Sacandaga and the old arrow-maker, and when they had gained the place they sought the latter broke the silence by saying,—

"It is now many days since I became aware that Sacandaga proposed to honor my poor lodge by a visit. Also am I informed of his object in coming, though he has told it to no man."

"How may such a thing be?" asked the other.

"To all men come dreams, but to a few only is given the power of understanding them," replied Kaweras. "The many dream dreams and forget them on waking. Some indeed recall them and make vain efforts to comprehend their meaning; but to Kaweras a dream speaks a language as easy of understanding as the signs of the forest or the voices of birds that dwell among its branches."

"So I have heard, and for that reason have I come to thee," said Sacandaga. "Tell me, then, what is my desire and if it may be accomplished."

"The Hurons are reported to be gathering on the war-path leading to the country of the Iroquois, and thy desire is to proceed with such promptness against them that they may be surprised and destroyed while still in their own territory. Then would you descend on their villages and wipe them out, that the power of our enemies may be broken forever."

"That is indeed a hope that I have cherished, but always in secret, and for my brother to know of it is proof that I have not done wrong in coming to him for advice," said Sacandaga. "How, then, Kaweras, will this plan of mine succeed, and shall we thus rid ourselves of the wolves whose howling has so long troubled our ears?"

The prophet hesitated before making reply. Then he said slowly, "Sometimes the dream-pictures are so plenty and come so quickly that it is hard to make out one from another, as it is hard to understand the words of one man when many are talking. I see a fight. In it are Maquas and Hurons. The Maquas chase their enemies and kill them. It is morning and the sun is shining. Also with this picture I see another battle in which the Hurons are overcoming the Maquas and taking many prisoners. In this one is thunder and lightning, by which many are killed. Which is the true picture I know not, nor how to advise my brother concerning them."

"Then will I interpret and tell thee their meaning," exclaimed Sacandaga. "Both are true, and their meaning is this. I and my young men are to go on the war-path against the Huron dogs and will surely encounter them. If we do so on a fair morning when there is no sign of storm in the air, then shall we overcome them and wipe them from the face of the earth. If we should meet them in the morning and delay an attack until later in the day, then would the Great Spirit grow angry and send his lightnings to destroy us. It is well, my brother. I will remember to seek the enemy on a fair morning and avoid him on a day of storm. Now I would ask thee one more question. What do thy dreams tell of the young man who is called Massasoit?"

"This only," answered Kaweras, "that he is the son of a chieftain, and will himself become a leader of men, wiser even and more powerful than his father."

"But who is his father?"

"I know not, though of late I have come to a suspicion that this young man may be Nahma, the missing son of Longfeather."

"That cannot be, for I have had dealings with the son of Longfeather and know that he and this youth are not one person."

"Did not that one also claim to be a son of Canonicus?"

"He did so claim."

"Then he may have spoken falsely; for Uncas, the Mohican, hath lately sent me word that Nahma and Miantinomo are two separate persons, holding no love for each other and having nothing in common."

"If the words of Uncas should prove true and it shall appear that I have been led falsely into a treaty with Canonicus, then shall the wrath of Sacandaga fall upon the Narragansetts even as one destroys a serpent that has stung him. I will look closely into the matter when I have returned from dealing with the Hurons. Until then it is well that I keep this young man where I may watch over him."

In the mean time the youth under discussion had just passed the pleasantest evening his short memory could recall. He was like a boy brought up in a nursery with only girls for companions, at length set free and for the first time admitted to the company of men. He had no recollection of companions of his own age and sex, so that the young warriors who now welcomed him to their ranks were revelations as surprising as they were interesting.

How much they knew, and what wonderful things they told him! At the same time how delightful was it to listen to their praise of his own accomplishments! Until now he had not known that he possessed accomplishments, but supposed that every one could shoot and run equally well with himself. He could not remember having learned to do these things, nor had he found occasion since entering the lodge of Kaweras to test his skill in them against that of others. Now, therefore, he was surprised as well as pleased to find himself in the position of a hero on account of abilities that he had heretofore regarded as commonplace.

So pleasant was the evening thus spent with his new companions that when Sacandaga gave the signal for conversation to cease that his young men might sleep and so prepare for an early start on the morrow, Nahma was filled with eager anticipations of the new life opening before him, and already wondered how he could have been content with that passed in the lodge of Kaweras.

With the earliest promise of dawn he was first of all the sleeping warriors to spring to his feet and begin preparations for departure. Such as he had to make were few and simple, but to him they were of vast importance. New moccasins and leggings of buckskin, a light robe of soft furs in which to wrap himself at night, and a wing feather from the great eagle for his head completed his list of personal belongings. Besides these he would take a bow and the quiver of fine flint-headed arrows that Kaweras presented to him that morning, his stone hatchet or tomahawk, and the copper scalping-knife that was his sole relic of a former but unremembered life. Also he must furnish to the general stock of provisions a large, close-woven basket of parched corn.

By sunrise a meal had been hastily eaten and everything was in readiness for the setting forth of the war-party. Kaweras embraced Nahma and bade him make for himself a name. Tears streamed down the cheeks of Otshata as she bade him farewell and pressed into his hands a pair of daintily embroidered moccasins as a token of remembrance. The youth looked on all sides for Aeana, but she was nowhere to be seen. Only after his canoe was well out on the river and he glanced back for a farewell view of the place that had been to him a home did he see, standing on a slight elevation and gazing in his direction, a solitary figure that he knew to be that of the girl who scorned him.

Some days later he found tucked down in the toe of one of Otshata's moccasins an exquisite little tinder-bag of softest fawn-skin that he had last seen hanging from the shapely neck of Aeana.

CHAPTER VIII

TWO YOUNG SCOUTS

For two days did Sacandaga's little expedition proceed up the Shate-muc, now making tedious carries around roaring waterfalls, and again laboriously hauling their laden canoes up some stretch of tumultuous rapids. At one of these places Sacandaga, bidding Nahma accompany him, left the river and made his way swiftly along a broad trail that led to the westward. After following it for a while they came to a place of many springs delightfully shaded by giant trees. Although no human being was to be seen, there were on all sides remnants of former encampments. Also the ground about certain of the springs was worn bare by innumerable hoof-prints, showing that deer and other animals were accustomed to gather here in great numbers. Deeply marked trails leading from every direction centred here, as though the springs formed a meeting-place for all people.

As Nahma noted these things Sacandaga smiled at his expression of astonishment. "It is Sara Tioga, the place of healing," he said. "To it come all who are sick or suffer pain that they may drink of the medicine waters and be cured. Many would be here now but for the report that an enemy is coming this way. When we have wiped him out then will we return hither, that we may rejoice with feasting and dancing. At that time will be seen a great gathering of the Iroquois, for this is the place of all their places that they most love. Now, however, we may tarry only long enough to drink of the life-giving waters and then must we hasten forward. In drinking take careful note of the spring most offensive to thy taste, for thus may be discovered which one is most needful to thy well-being."

So Nahma drank of all the springs, finding some of them salt, some sparkling with effervescence, and others so nauseous that he turned from them in disgust.

"I like none of them and will drink no more," he finally declared.

"Then must all of them be for thy good and thou must stand in need of all the elements they contain," answered his companion, who cared to hear naught but praise of his beloved springs. "But let us go, for we have no time to lose."

As they turned to depart from the beautiful place, Nahma suddenly sprang upon his companion with such violence that Sacandaga was hurled to the ground and the young man fell with him. At the same moment an arrow was buried to its shaft in the trunk of a beech a few paces in front of them, where it stood quivering with the force that had sped it. Even as he fell Nahma bounded up, and an instant later, when the startled sachem also gained his feet, he saw the young warrior darting back in the direction from which they had just come.

At the same time a third figure hideously daubed with war-paint appeared in plain view. He stood directly in front of the rash youth with bended bow and a second arrow drawn to its head. Quick as thought Nahma dropped, and the feathered missile flew harmlessly above him. As he again leaped to his feet his assailant turned to fly, but ere he had taken half a dozen steps he sprang convulsively into the air and plunged headlong with outstretched arms. An arrow sped from Sacandaga's bow had passed through his body.

"Why did you kill him?" asked Nahma, regretfully, as the two stood together looking down on the still twitching body of their late foe.

"Is it not what my young brother would have done?" inquired Sacandaga, in surprise.

"No; I would have caught him and made him tell me things."

"What things?"

"Why he hid from us and tried to kill us, who he was, and what he was doing here. I do not remember seeing him among thy young men."

Sacandaga smiled grimly. "He seems to have escaped being seen until he came within range of Quick-eye's vision; but all thy questions may be answered in a word. He is a Huron."

"A Huron!" cried Nahma. "How may that be, when he looks like other men? I thought a Huron was a wolf. Surely my father has said so."

"A Huron is a wolf in spirit," replied Sacandaga, as he stooped and deftly removed the dead man's scalp, "but the wolfish spirit is concealed beneath the semblance of a man."

"Then how may one know a Huron?" asked the puzzled youth.

"By his paint, his moccasins, the cut of his scalp-lock, the fashion of his weapons, his cast of feature, and by a thousand other signs as plain as the difference between light and darkness."

All these things had once been well known to Nahma; but now they were as though he had never before heard of them, and he listened eagerly to the words of Sacandaga's lesson.

"This time," concluded the sachem, "my young brother has done well, and to his quickness of sight combined with promptness of action do I owe my life. But never again, my son, run openly upon an enemy without first knowing his strength. It is seldom that a Huron spy comes alone into the Iroquois country, and had there been others, or even one other, with this one, thy death had been certain. Always when surprised seek first a place of hiding from which to discover the strength of thy enemy and plan for meeting him."

The Huron scout who had just paid the penalty of his daring was one of two sent to discover if the Iroquois had knowledge concerning the projected invasion of their country. His companion had remained with their canoe at the upper end of Andia-ta-roc-te (Lake George) while he had penetrated the country as far as the springs of healing, where, if the Iroquois felt themselves secure from invasion, he was certain to discover a number of their lodges. He was greatly disappointed at finding the place unoccupied, and was about to retrace his steps with the information that an alarm had been given, when Sacandaga and his young companion appeared on the scene. Hiding like a snake in the grass, the Huron watched these two with longing eyes while waiting to see if they would be followed by others. He recognized Sacandaga, and was determined if possible to carry back with him the scalp of that redoubtable chieftain.

An opportunity came as his enemies turned to depart, and he cautiously brought his bow into position. At that instant Nahma, glancing back, caught sight of a tip of the weapon projecting above the tall grasses and did the only thing possible to save his companion's life.

As the fortunate survivors of this episode left the scene of its occurrence they took a path leading northward, and after a time came again to the Sha-temuc, having cut off a great bend of the river that the canoes must necessarily follow. As they went they discovered the slight trail left by the Huron scout, but at the river it was lost. Wading to the opposite bank, Nahma soon recovered it, and asked permission to follow it farther; but Sacandaga would not grant this until the arrival of the canoes. Then, after briefly relating what had happened, he selected a young warrior already famous as a trailer and ordered him to accompany Nahma over the path the Huron had come. This warrior was named Ah-mik-pan-pin, or the Grinning Beaver, on account of two prominent front teeth over which his lips were never wholly closed.

"Have a care," said Sacandaga on parting with the young men, "and run no risks for the sake of scalps. What I desire is a knowledge of the party to which that Huron belonged. I would know how large it is, where it is camped, and whether it is coming or going. Find out these things as quickly as may be and come again with thy news. The Maquas will sleep to-night at the foot of the great rock by the shore of the wide waters. They will have no fire and will make no sound, but he who utters the cry of wah-o-nai-sa (the whippoorwill) twice and then once will be answered by the same cry once and then twice. Go thou and come again quickly."

With this Nahma and Grinning Beaver set forth, and were instantly lost to view in the thickness of the forest. For two hours they sped forward without a pause, then they began to see spaces of light through the trees, and the Beaver intimated that they must now exercise the greatest caution.

"This trail will not lead us to them," he whispered, "for they will have moved to one side or the other after their runner left. Let us, then, go separately to the water's edge, thou on the one side and I on the other. Whoever reaches the beach first shall utter the cry of wah-o-nai-sa, and if it be not quickly answered he shall return to see what is wrong. Is it well?"

"It is well," replied Nahma, and the two went their respective ways as agreed.

With the utmost caution and without a sound louder than his own breathing did Nahma circle towards the lighted space marking the limit of the forest. All at once he stopped and listened. From behind him, faint and distant, he had heard an unmistakable exclamation of surprise.

It was not repeated nor did he hear further sounds, but it was enough, and after a moment of listening he started back over the way he had come. He found the place where he had parted from his companion, and then followed the slight trail made by the latter. Suddenly and without warning he came upon a sight so startling that he stood in his tracks like one petrified, gazing at it with dilated eyes.

Two warriors locked in a deadly embrace lay motionless on the ground. Their surroundings were drenched with blood, and to all appearance both were dead. Nahma stooped over them, and saw to his horror that one of the faces, so swollen and distorted that he had not sooner recognized it, was that of his recent comrade. The other was a Huron, and a knife still clutched by the Beaver's hand was buried to the hilt in his heart. At the same time his own fingers held the throat of the young Iroquois with a grip like that of a vise.

It required all of Nahma's strength to unlock that death-clutch, but at length he succeeded, and the two mortal foes so recently thrilled with vigorous life lay side by side stark and rigid.

CHAPTER IX

ON THE LAKE

Nahma gazed about him in dismay. Night was coming on, he was alone in a place of which he had no knowledge, and he believed himself surrounded by enemies. He even fancied he could see dark faces peering at him from behind the shadowy tree-trunks. Above all, the companion upon whom he had relied for guidance and counsel lay dead at his feet. Although a savage himself, accustomed only to savage sights and ways, our lad had seen so little of death that this last fact seemed incredible. He kneeled beside the Beaver and gazed into his face, calling him by name in a low voice and bidding him open his eyes.

As he did this the dreadful aspect of the face on which he was looking suggested another that he had seen but a week earlier. It had been that of a man drowned in the Shatemuc and brought to the lodge of Kaweras. To all appearance he was dead, and yet the old arrow-maker had restored him to life. Nahma remembered perfectly what was done at that time, for he had closely watched every operation, and had even assisted Kaweras in his efforts. Now, in his despair over the present situation, but feeling that he could not yield to it without making some attempt at its betterment, he set to work upon the Beaver exactly as Kaweras had done with the drowned man. He turned the body on its face, drew forward the tongue, and cleared the mouth of froth. Then by rolling the body on its side and back again, at the same time applying a gentle pressure to back and breast, he forced air into and expelled it again from the lungs, thus producing an artificial breathing. After that he sought to restore circulation by rubbing upward along the legs. In all his efforts he was without hope of success and only worked for the sake of doing something. He was therefore utterly amazed as well as overjoyed to detect in his patient a slight gasping for breath. He could scarcely believe he had heard aright until it was repeated, and then he knew that the Beaver was still to be counted among those who lived.

Without thought of the danger from probable enemies, Nahma sprang to his feet, started towards the lake for water, and had gone half-way before he recalled that he had nothing in which to fetch it. Upon this he ran back, and picking up the still unconscious form of his companion, staggered to the beach with it in his arms. On his way he ran across a canoe concealed in a clump of bushes, but paid no attention to it for the moment.

As he laid his burden on the sand and glanced up to see if they were still safe from the presence of enemies, he detected a vague form some distance up the beach that disappeared within the forest even as he looked. It must of course be a Huron warrior, and doubtless others were with him. In that case to remain where they were meant certain destruction, and there was but one way to save his helpless companion as well as himself. The canoe that he had just discovered would at least bear them away from the treacherous forest and give them a fighting chance for their lives in the open.

In another minute Nahma had launched the light craft, placed his comrade inside, and was paddling furiously out over the lake. He had not gone more than one hundred yards when a series of yells from behind, and a flight of arrows sent with deadly intent, showed that his escape was discovered. Most of the arrows fell short, and none of them inflicted any damage. At the same time Nahma, glancing back, thought he saw other canoes coming down the coast.

It was now so nearly dark that all objects were indistinct, and if he could only maintain his lead for a short time longer he might still evade his pursuers. So the tired youth infused new energy into his paddling and urged his craft forward with redoubled speed. As he knew nothing of the lake, he had no idea where to look for the great rock beside which Sacandaga was to spend the night, nor was the Beaver in any condition to afford him information. So he held a course as far as possible from both shores and continued his paddling until nearly midnight, when he was forced by sheer exhaustion to give it over.

Dark as was the night, our lad could still distinguish the darker forms of occasional islands as he passed them, and at length drawing cautiously in towards one of these, he made a landing. In all this time the Beaver had been slowly struggling back to life, but he was still devoid of strength or a knowledge of his surroundings. So Nahma prepared as well as he could a bed of branches and grass, to which he bore his comrade. He also dragged up the canoe and turned it on its side to provide shelter from a drizzle of chill rain that was beginning to fall. Having completed these simple preparations, the youth ate a handful of parched corn drawn from his wallet, and lying down beside the Beaver was almost instantly fast asleep.

In regard to the necessaries of life the American of that day was in no degree removed from the beasts of the field. Like them he could thrive upon the natural products of the forest, and he also found its shelters sufficient for his needs even in the most inclement weather. With materials for a feast at hand he feasted; but when they were lacking he went without food uncomplainingly and for incredible lengths of time. If in the present instance our lad had dared allow himself the luxury of a fire he would quickly have acquired all the comforts of a home, including an abundance of cooked food, a good bed, warmth, and light. As it was he accepted cold, wet, hunger, and a most uncomfortable resting-place as things liable to be encountered at any time in the ordinary course of events.

The remainder of the night passed without incident, and by dawn Nahma was once more alert. His first move was to climb a tall tree that stood close at hand and take a comprehensive survey of the lake. Seeing it thus for the first time by daylight, he was impressed by its marvellous beauty. Its blue waters were dotted with islands all wooded and blending every shade of green. On both sides forest-covered hills rose abruptly from the shore, and back of them towered mountains higher than any he had ever seen. The lake was nowhere more than a mile or two in width, and to the northward it narrowed rapidly.

Having gazed as long as he dared on the outspread beauties of the scene, and satisfied himself that nothing was in motion on the face of the waters, the youth descended from his observatory and proceeded to make ready a breakfast. He was tired of parched corn, and his ravenous appetite demanded something more substantial. He even decided to run the risk of a fire. So he gathered a small quantity of dry, hard wood that would burn with the least amount of smoke, and, after an exasperating struggle with flints and tinder, caught a spark that was finally fanned into a brisk blaze. With the making of a fire the hardest part of his breakfast-getting was ended, although he had as yet nothing to cook. Five minutes later, however, he was in possession of a large pickerel and two good-sized bass, all of which had been enticed within striking distance of his arrows by a bait of worms. These fish wrapped in green leaves were buried under a bed of coals, and while they were cooking Nahma gathered berries.

When all was in readiness, he was vastly disappointed to find that his companion was unable to share in the meal. The Beaver had so far recovered that he was able to sit up and take an intelligent interest in what was going on. The expression of longing with which he regarded those baked fish left no doubt that he, too, was hungry; but, alas! he could not swallow food. His throat was so swollen that he could not even speak, and he still breathed with difficulty. He was so parched with thirst that he managed after a painful struggle to swallow a few drops of water, but that was all.

So Nahma was reluctantly obliged to eat alone while his companion watched him enviously. As he ate, the former told what he knew concerning the events of the preceding evening, and the Beaver learned for the first time that they were on an island far down the lake in hiding from a war-party of Hurons. He had wondered at finding himself alone with Nahma instead of in Sacandaga's company, but had supposed that they were within a short distance of the great rock, as he knew had been the case when they first gained the lake-shore. His distress at being unable to ask questions and express his views on the situation was so evident as to suggest a possible remedy, upon which Nahma immediately set to work. First he stripped some sheets of bark from a white birch, and with them fashioned a rude but water-tight bowl that would hold about a gallon. This he partially filled with water. In the mean time he had thrown into the fire some large beach pebbles, and these were now thoroughly heated. Lifting them with forked sticks and dropping them into the bowl, he almost instantly had hot water, with which he bade the Beaver bathe his throat.

While the latter was doing this Nahma bethought himself to climb once more into his observatory for another look at the lake. As he gained the highest available branch and glanced back over the way they had come he uttered an exclamation of dismay. Not more than two miles distant was a fleet of canoes advancing directly towards him. He could plainly see the flash of their paddles and note their movements as they separated or closed together. There was no doubt but that the enemy from whom he had fled was again close upon him, and to remain on that island meant certain discovery, since no Indian would pass a fire without finding out by whom it had been kindled. To leave the island and make for the mainland on either side was out of the question, for their moving canoe would surely be discovered. Thus the only thing remaining to be done was to proceed straight down the lake, with the hope of gaining another place of concealment while still hidden by the island from those who came behind.

With this plan formed our young warrior hastily descended the tree, told his companion that the Hurons were again in hot pursuit, and bundled him into the canoe ere he had time to gain further information. Then Nahma gave him a paddle and told him that if he valued his life he must put forth whatever of strength he had remaining.

CHAPTER X

AN OKI OF THE WATERS

As Nahma had intended remaining on the island until his companion fully recovered from his injuries, he had not hurried with anything that he had done that morning. Consequently it was mid-day when the flight was resumed and the fugitives again headed their canoe down the lake, keeping the island directly behind them as a screen from their pursuers. Although working furiously at his paddle, Nahma glanced behind him every few moments, and as time passed was amazed that the enemy did not come into sight.

At length, after a couple of hours of incessant labor, the canoe rounded a bold headland that nearly cut the lake in twain, and was hidden behind it from any who might be following. Here the lake was very narrow, and Nahma proposed that they should run the canoe ashore, hide it, and seek to rejoin their friends by land.

"No," said the Beaver, who had recovered his power of speech. "If the Hurons are following us, they will surely have scouts in the forest on both sides. We should be certain to fall in with these, and I am not yet ready for fighting. Now that we have come thus far by water, let us keep on. At a short distance from here this lake ends, but it is joined to another much larger. On that other a canoe may go north even to the country of the Hurons. It may also go south to the land of the Iroquois. Let us, then, find the big water and turn to the south, for if those following us be Hurons they will certainly hold a course to the northward."

"We will do as my brother says," replied Nahma, delighted to have again the counsel of his more experienced companion. So the course of the canoe was continued, but only Nahma now wielded a paddle. The Beaver had been so much benefited by hot-water applications and by the subsequent exercise of paddling that his throat was again serviceable. Not only could he talk but he believed he could eat, and as Nahma had brought along one of the three fish caught for breakfast, he made the attempt with such gratifying success that it quickly disappeared. Being thus refreshed and strengthened, he began to question his companion concerning the events of the preceding night.

When Nahma related the finding of the two mortal enemies clutched in a death-grapple the Beaver said,—

"It is so. As I saw the Huron he saw me, and we sprang at each other with our knives, for we were too close to use bows or even the tomahawk. His knife broke, and as I drove mine into his body his fingers closed about my throat. Ugh! It was the grip of a bear, and I could not loose it. Again and again did I bury my knife in his heart, but he would not let go. Then all became black and I died. How my brother brought me back from the place of Okis [departed spirits] I know not, but when next I awoke he lay beside me under a canoe and a band as of fire was about my head. Now, therefore, the life of Grinning Beaver belongs to his brother. But tell me quickly how knew you we were pursued by Hurons? There were traces of but two of them, while many of our own people were to meet Sacandaga at the great rock."

"I know that our pursuers are Hurons, or at least enemies, because they crept on us by stealth. Also when they saw we had escaped they yelled with rage and shot arrows to kill us. Besides that, they followed after us in canoes, and but for the coming of darkness would surely have overtaken us."

"Is it certain that they shot after us with arrows?"

"It is certain, for one of them struck the canoe and lies even yet where it fell. So my brother may see for himself and know that I have spoken truly."

The Beaver plucked the arrow thus indicated from the sheathing of the canoe in which its point was embedded and examined it closely. As he did so a puzzled expression came over his face, and he exclaimed,—

"But this is not a Huron arrow! It is of the Iroquois, and might have been made by Kaweras himself. Look. As a bowman thou shouldst know this fashion of feathering."

"I do know it," replied Nahma, taking the proffered arrow as he spoke and studying its make. "Also I should have recognized it sooner had I looked, but it fell in darkness, and since then I have been too busy to recall it until now."

"If this was the only style of arrow aimed at us," continued the Beaver, "those who pursue us must be friends, who have in turn mistaken us for enemies."

"It would seem so," agreed Nahma, in a mortified tone, "and it is to my shame that I should have shown so great stupidity."

"Take it not to heart, my brother. No warrior may learn his trade save by experience. What you have done has been well done, and no harm has come of it. Only now that we know those behind us to be friends, we must look sharply for enemies in front and see that our friends come not upon them unaware."

"Shall we not turn back at once," asked Nahma, "and give to Sacandaga a warning of the true state of affairs?"

"Not at once, but presently," replied the Beaver, "for we are even now close to the great waters of which I spoke. It will be well, therefore, if we take a look at them before turning back. We may thus have news to report that will cause him to rejoice at sight of us."

During this conversation Nahma had continued to paddle easily, and the canoe had glided gently forward with the current of a forest-shaded stream forming an outlet to the lake they had just traversed. As the Beaver concluded his remarks the roar of falling waters ahead of them gave warning that their farther progress in this direction was barred. So the canoe was left cunningly as though it had drifted to that place, and the two young scouts made their way through a mile-wide strip of forest to the shore of a second lake that lay behind. Here they gazed eagerly out over the wide water-way, but for a moment saw nothing unusual. As they were about to venture into the open, Nahma checked the movement with a guarded exclamation of amazement. A human figure had suddenly appeared on the crest of a headland that jutted into the lake a short distance from them, and for several seconds it stood motionless in the full light of the westering sun, as though spell-bound by the beauty of the outspread landscape.

Although it presented the form of man, it was unlike anything either of the astonished observers had ever seen. It appeared twice the size of an ordinary man, and at certain points it glinted in the sunlight with a sheen like that of rippling waters. Its head, upon which the sunlight also flashed, was of huge proportions and apparently devoid of hair.

"It is an Oki," whispered the Beaver, apprehensively. "A god of the waters. See you not how he shines with wetness?"

Even as the Beaver spoke, a second figure appeared for an instant beside the one at which the awe-stricken youths were gazing. It was that of a man like themselves, half-naked, painted, and bedecked with feathers. This last apparition plucked the other by the arm and they disappeared together.

Our young scouts looked at each other in wonderment. "We must know more of this affair," said the Beaver. "Let us move in that direction and see what may be found."

A few minutes later, moving with the utmost caution, they had reached a point from which they could look beyond the headland. There they beheld a scene that held their gaze with breathless interest, and, crouching beneath the overhanging branches of a thick-growing spruce, they watched it in silence.

The sun was setting and its light was growing dim, but they could see a fleet of canoes drawn up on the lake-shore, and beyond them many men moving busily about a large cleared space. They could not discover among these the strange figure that had first attracted their attention, nor was there any glow of fire-light.

The Beaver drew in his breath as though about to speak, but Nahma checked him with warning hand, and at the same instant a twig snapped directly behind them. The young scouts dared not so much as move their heads, but from the corners of their eyes they caught glimpses of four shadowy forms that flitted noiselessly by and vanished in the direction from which they themselves had come. They were Hurons seeking to make certain before the complete shutting in of night that no enemy lurked in the vicinity of their camp.

For several minutes after these had passed our lads remained motionless and silent. Then the Beaver rose and moved without a sound in the direction taken by the Huron scouts, while Nahma, his nerves tense with excitement, followed the lead thus given. Neither spoke until finally they came again to the place where they had left their canoe. To their dismay, it was gone, but the Beaver said in a whisper,—

"It is well for us that it is of Huron make, so that they may think it was left by those of their own people who were sent ahead. Now let us find Sacandaga, for we have much to tell him."

The task of making their unlit way back along the shore of the stream they had so recently descended without effort was beset with many difficulties. They must keep close to the river, for not only was it their guide but by it sooner or later their friends were almost certain to pass. They must thread the forest mazes in silence, and they must pause with every minute to listen for the dip of paddles. Even then Sacandaga's canoes might drift by them unseen and unheard. But a warning must be given, if such a thing were possible, and in spite of all obstacles they pushed steadily forward.

At length they came to a place where the stream began to broaden. They had gained the lower end of Andia-ta-roc-te and dared go no farther. So they waited while Nahma uttered full and clear the plaintive call of the whippoorwill. Twice did he repeat it, and then once more after a brief interval.

CHAPTER XI

THE COMING OF SACANDAGA

As the concluding notes of Nahma's cry echoed over the still waters and were lost among the distant hills, the two youths listened anxiously for an answer. Nor had they long to wait, for within a minute the call of a whippoorwill came back to them almost exactly as the young warrior had uttered it; but it came from the wrong direction.

"Sacandaga has passed us after all," muttered Nahma in a tone of vexation.

"Not so," replied the Beaver, "for that was not the answer agreed upon. Do you not remember? The call was to be two and then one, while the answer was to be one and then two. This answer came back even as the call was given, and so could not have been made by Sacandaga or any of his warriors."

"Who, then——?" began Nahma, but he was interrupted by a quavering note of ko-ko-anse (the little screech-owl) that came from no great distance.

"It is a Huron call," whispered the Beaver; "answer it quickly." This Nahma did, and the Beaver continued, "They are on the water and will come to this point for further information. Do you remain here and take care that they discover not thy presence. I will retire a little and entice them or some of them to me, for I can speak the Huron tongue. After that we must be guided by what will follow. Is it well?"

"It is well," whispered Nahma, as he crouched low beside a log, one end of which extended into the water. He did not hear the Beaver take his departure, but knew that he was gone. Then from off the river, but close at hand, came again the tremulous cry of ko-ko-anse. It was answered by the Beaver from a short distance inland, who in a voice disguised as though by weakness cried,—

"Help me, brothers. Help me before I die."

"Who calls?" inquired a voice from the water.

"A Huron scout sorely wounded and helpless," answered the Beaver.

"Is he alone?"

"He is alone. There was another with him, but he was killed two days since. Help or I perish."

"Art thou Chebacno or Wabensickewa?"

"I am Wabensickewa. Chebacno was slain by the Iroquois, who are even now making ready a war-party. I hastened back to bring news of it, and landed here to rest until darkness. While I slept a panther leaped on my back. Before I could kill him he had so injured me that I cannot walk. Also are my eyes blinded so that I cannot see. I have a canoe that you will find at the water's edge, if indeed the wind has not drifted it away. I have called many times, and was about to give over calling when your answer came to lend me new strength. Now, then, my brothers, come quickly, for I have much to tell before I die."

A moment later Nahma felt a slight jar pass through the log against which he lay and heard a few whispered words of consultation. Then two figures stepped ashore and, passing so close to him that he could have touched them, noiselessly entered the forest. He waited for a moment and then cautiously lifted his head. Against the faint gleam of water he could distinguish the black bulk of a canoe and see that it still held two other figures who sat motionless. Slowly he raised his bow with a stone-headed arrow fitted to its string until one of the sitting figures was fairly covered. Then he waited with tense muscles and a heart that seemed like to burst with its furious beating. From behind him came a low moaning that he knew was made by the Beaver to deceive his enemies.

Suddenly the oppressive silence was broken by the twang of a bowstring that was instantly followed by fierce yells. High above these rose the defiant war-cry of the Iroquois, but its last note was cut short and ended in a choking gurgle.

Somehow Nahma managed to hear these things, though he was at the same time intensely busy with affairs of his own. At the first intimation of a struggle behind him he had let fly his ready arrow, and one of the two figures in the canoe dropped heavily forward. The other, seeing what he had supposed was a log suddenly endowed with life and leaping towards him, uttered a cry of terror, sprang overboard, and disappeared beneath the black waters. While Nahma tossed the limp form of the other Huron from the canoe preparatory to going in pursuit of this swimmer, a rustling among the bushes warned him to make good his own escape while yet he might, and giving the canoe a great shove, he leaped aboard.

As the craft shot out into the open a voice hailed it from the shore; but as the words were spoken in the Huron tongue, Nahma made no answer. He hesitated for a moment, wondering whether it might not be the Beaver who called; but with a repetition of the demand he knew that that was not the case. He was confirmed in this belief by hearing a slight splash from close at hand, a stifled exclamation, and a few whispered words. Evidently the swimmer who had made so hasty an exit from the canoe had been encouraged by the voice of a friend to gain the land, and now the two were once more in communication.

What had become of the Beaver? Recalling the Iroquois war-cry and its sadly suggestive ending, Nahma had little doubt that he had been overcome and killed. He hated to think of deserting his comrade without knowing for a certainty whether he were alive or dead, and yet to attempt a landing in face of two enemies, and perhaps three, would be an act of folly. His canoe had drifted out so far that they could not see him in his present position, but it would be almost impossible to gain the shore anywhere in that vicinity without detection.

While in this state of indecision, which in reality lasted but a few seconds, he heard faint and far away the cry of a whippoorwill. Twice was it uttered, and then again after a short interval. It must be the signal of Sacandaga, since it came from up the lake. Doubtless it had been made in answer to the Beaver's far-reaching war-cry. In another moment Nahma's canoe, impelled by a noiseless paddle, was speeding in that direction. He dared not at once reply to the signal for fear of drawing a flight of Huron arrows; but as soon as he believed himself beyond range of these he rested on his paddle and sent far across the lake the vibrant cry of wah-o-nai-sa once and then twice.

A full minute elapsed before the answer came, and then he was startled by its nearness. Had he not known better, he would have sworn that it was uttered by a bird in flight while passing directly above him. Allowing his craft to drift, he listened and heard the quick dip of many paddles. A fleet of canoes was rushing towards him, and, as he began to distinguish their vague outlines, he uttered a low call to attract attention.

"Who is it?" demanded the voice of Sacandaga, sharply, as the speed of the oncoming canoes was checked.

"It is Massasoit," answered the lad.

"Where is Grinning Beaver, thy companion? Did he utter the war-cry of the Iroquois that came to us as we were entering our canoes for a night of travel?"

"I fear the Beaver is dead," replied Nahma. "And if so, he was killed even with the sounding of his war-cry."

"Who killed him?" demanded Sacandaga, fiercely.

"The Hurons."

"How many are there?"

"Only four did we encounter. Of these I saw one fall, and believe that the Beaver, who was separated from me, killed another. One leaped into the water and one I know escaped from the Beaver."

"Were you on land or on the water?"

"We were on land, and this is the canoe in which the Hurons came."

"Where did it happen?"

"At the beginning of a river that leads to the wide waters lying towards the rising sun."

"What know you of these wide waters? Have you been to them?"

"Shortly before the coming of darkness were we there, and we turned back to bring news of the war-party that we saw."

"Hurons?"

"Hurons, my father, and like the leaves of a tree for numbers. Also they have with them an Oki to make timid the hearts of their enemies."

"What mean you by an Oki?"

With this Nahma described as well as he could the strange being seen by himself and the Beaver, and all who could get within hearing listened to his words with breathless attention. When Nahma declared that the apparition, though seen on a headland, still gleamed with wetness as though just emerged from the lake, his auditors were deeply impressed. Only Sacandaga was incredulous, and appeared to treat the incident as of small account.

"It is but a Huron trick!" he exclaimed, that all might hear. "They are too cowardly to fight like men, but have prepared an image with the hope that sight of it will turn our blood to water. It is well, though, that we have learned of this thing and know what to expect. Now let us find whether the Beaver is alive or dead, and if the Huron dogs have indeed slain him, bitterly shall he be avenged before we are done with them."

So Nahma guided the Iroquois canoes to the place where he had uttered that first fateful call of the whippoorwill, and Sacandaga, with half a dozen warriors, made a landing on the very log beside which he had lain.

It took them but a few minutes to discover the body of their late comrade cold in death and scalped; but there was no trace of those who had perpetrated the deed. If he had indeed killed one of them, the others had either hidden the body or taken it away.

Having learned these things and thirsting for vengeance, the Iroquois re-entered their canoes and glided silently down-stream towards the place where their enemies were encamped.

CHAPTER XII

A MEETING OF DEADLY FOES

After carrying their canoes around the two waterfalls that obstruct the outlet of Lake George, the Iroquois finally glided like so many night-shadows out onto the surface of Lake Champlain. Then, guided by the son of Long-feather, they approached the place where he had seen the Hurons. Sacandaga had entered the canoe of the young scout that he might learn more fully what had happened during the past two days; also his place was in the leading canoe, that from it he might direct the movements of his followers, who were now nearly two hundred in number.

He had thought of attempting a night surprise of the northern invaders by attacking their camp under cover of darkness; but this plan was dismissed almost as soon as formed, for he remembered the prophecy of Kaweras. The fight in which the Iroquois were to be successful must take place in broad daylight and on a fair morning. The battle might not, therefore, be waged at night, nor even on the morrow, unless it were a day of cloudless sunshine. At the same time the Hurons must be given no chance for escape, and to compel them to remain where they were he stationed his force at the mouth of the cove in which lay their fleet. This position was taken in silence and, it was thought, without attracting attention.

That the men from the north had, however, received notice of their enemies' coming and were keenly on the alert to meet them was soon proved by a jeering hail from the land.

"Are the bark-eaters fish that they remain in the water? If they call themselves men, why do they not come on shore and accept the welcome awaiting them?"

To this taunt the Iroquois replied with a chorus of fierce yells and savage intimations of what would happen when they got ready to enter the camp of the Huron dogs.

So the night was spent in a brisk exchange of taunts, jeers, threats, and insulting remarks well calculated to increase the bitterness of the hate already existing between the two tribes. The Iroquois even betrayed their knowledge of the mysterious being whom the Hurons had called to their aid, and expressed the utmost contempt for him. To this those on shore made no reply except to advise the Iroquois to call upon their own gods for the aid they would surely need on the morrow.

"Something has given them courage," remarked Sacandaga, "for never have I known Hurons to talk so bravely in the presence of Iroquois. But we will see whether their boldness can stand the test of daylight."

At length the wished-for dawn arrived, and by its earliest gleams Sacandaga landed his force at a point beyond arrow-shot of the Huron camp and bade them light fires for the preparation of breakfast. He was well aware of the fighting value of a full stomach, and was too wise a leader not to seek every possible advantage even against a foe whom he despised.

Nor were the Hurons less ready to make the most of this opportunity for preparing cooked food, the first time they had dared do so in several days. Thus both parties remained hidden from each other, except through the eyes of their watchful scouts, until the sun was an hour high. Not only did Sacandaga wish to refresh his men by this rest, but he was determined not to begin fighting until assured of conditions propitious to his undertaking. With the weather, however, he had every reason to be pleased, for never was a fairer morn. The sky was cloudless, the air clear and crisp, the lake of a heavenly blue, and all nature was at its best. As he looked about him he became elated over the certainty of his forthcoming victory.

"The Hurons have never yet been able to stand before an equal number of Iroquois," he said, "and to-day with all things in our favor it will be strange indeed if we do not wipe them out. But we may not delay, lest the spirits become angry and send their lightnings to punish our indifference to the favors they have shown. Let us, then, get to work and finish this business quickly, that we may the more speedily return to our own people."

Although Sacandaga was one of the most skilful warriors of his time, and well versed in all the tricks of his trade as practised by forest fighters, he saw fit in the present instance to lead his painted savages to the attack in a compact body. As the Hurons occupied the centre of a large cleared space so wide as to place them beyond the reach of arrows from forest covers, this plan was in a measure forced upon him. At the same time he hoped to overawe the enemy and terrify him by the number and ferocious appearance of his followers. So the Iroquois, half naked, painted, befeathered, decked with bears' claws and wolf-tails, dashed from the forest yelling and brandishing their weapons, and advanced with a rush to where the Hurons awaited them.

The latter appeared terrified, and seemed to shrink from the impending onslaught. Then their solid formation broke, leaving a wide gap, from which stepped a single figure. The Iroquois were not more than fifty paces distant; but at sight of this apparition they came to a sudden halt and stood as though petrified with amazement. The figure confronting them was indeed that described by Massasoit, only it loomed up larger than they had expected, and gleamed with a dazzling lustre in the bright sunlight. It had the form of a man, but its face was covered with a growth of hair that hung down on its breast.

The person who appeared so remarkable to the denizens of the forest that they deemed him a god was none other than the intrepid French explorer Samuel de Champlain, founder of the city of Quebec. With but two followers he had been induced to accompany a war-party of Canadian Indians on their foray into Iroquois territory, and was thus the first of his race to look upon the waters of the noble lake that has ever since borne his name.

For a few moments the Iroquois gazed awe-stricken upon this first white man they had ever seen. Then, relying upon the prophecy of Kaweras, that only thunder and lightning could prevent them from winning a victory, they bent their bows and let fly a cloud of arrows. Many of these were aimed at the white man standing so boldly before them, but, to their dismay, he remained unharmed. Nahma in particular, who had shot at the very centre of the shining breastplate, was amazed and terrified to see his arrow, after striking, bound back as though it had encountered a wall of rock.

But scant time was given for the consideration of this marvel; for, even as they shot at him, the mysterious being brought into position a strange-looking stick that he carried until it was pointed directly at them. Then came a flash of lightning, a roar of thunder, a cloud of smoke, and a dozen of the Iroquois fell to the ground as though smitten by the wrath of God. As was afterwards proved, but two of them were killed and one—Sacandaga—was grievously wounded, while the others had fallen from sheer fright. At the same time the Hurons rushed forward with triumphant yells and a flight of arrows.

For a moment the Iroquois wavered and seemed about to fly. Then Nahma, son of Longfeather, sprang to the front with a loud cry, and, swinging a stone war-club above his head, made straight for the thunder-god who had wrought such havoc. Champlain was in the act of drawing his sword when he was staggered by a terrific blow that would surely have killed him but for the steel cap that he wore. Before he could recover, and ere a second blow could be delivered, there came another flash of lightning accompanied by its thunderous roar from a clump of bushes at one side, and two more Iroquois were stricken with sudden death.

At this fresh proof that the all-powerful spirits were indeed fighting against them the hearts of the Iroquois melted, and they fled from the field a panic-stricken mob. Even Nahma joined in the mad flight; but he paused long enough to pick up his wounded chieftain, whom he hoped to be able to carry as far as the canoes.

At their heels streamed the exultant Hurons, striking down the fugitives by the score. One of these drove a spear through the body of Sacandaga; and

Nahma, staggering under his burden, was knocked down by the force of the blow. As he disengaged himself from the dead sachem and regained his feet he found himself once more face to face with the awful being who held in his hands the thunders and lightning of a Manitou.

At this moment Champlain, who had found time to reload his musket, fired a second shot into the ranks of the flying Iroquois. Ere its smoke could lift, Nahma, frenzied with rage and reckless of consequences, sprang upon the white man with uplifted knife. The blow was urged with all the splendid strength of the young warrior's arm, but it only bent the copper blade in his grasp and left him defenceless. Ere he could renew his flight he was flung to the earth and bound immovably with thongs of tough bark.

Nahma's first battle was ended in utter defeat, but he did not feel humiliated, for he believed that he had fought against immortal spirits who could come to no harm from the hands of man. He only wondered vaguely, as he lay awaiting the pleasure of his captors, why the Okis should have ranged themselves on the side of the perfidious Hurons instead of aiding the Iroquois, whom he then believed to be the most nearly perfect of human beings.

About one-half the force that Sacandaga had led so confidently to battle that morning reached the canoes and continued their flight up the lake. The Hurons did not pursue them, for they were too busy killing or taking captive those who were left behind.

By noon the whole affair was ended, and the triumphant Hurons, taking with them twoscore of dejected prisoners, as many bloody Iroquois scalps, and a number of canoes laden with spoils, set forth on their return to the St. Lawrence.

With them went Champlain, still thrilled with the excitement of fighting and killing, but already disgusted with the barbarities of his savage allies. Could he have foreseen that his act of that day had created a powerful enemy who for two hundred years to come would let pass no opportunity for the killing of a Frenchman, his thoughts would have been still more sombre.

In camp that night, while still occupied with his melancholy reflections, he was accosted by one of his white companions, who said,—

"Look yonder, monsieur. They are about to punish in pretty fashion the young devil who twice this day attempted to take thy life."

CHAPTER XIII

TO THE LODGES OF THE WHITE MAN

Realizing that for some reason the all-powerful white man who had that day given them a victory over their enemies was displeased, the Hurons agreed after a long consultation that it must be because the only one among the Iroquois who had dared attack him was still allowed to live. So, although such pleasures were generally reserved for their home-returning, they determined to sacrifice the audacious young warrior on the spot with the hope of thus regaining the favor of their allies. In order that he might thoroughly comprehend what was in store for him, they decided that he should first witness the torture of one of his companions. For this purpose a victim was selected at random from among the captives, and the two young men, facing each other, were securely bound to saplings standing but a few yards apart.

About the feet of each was piled a quantity of dry wood, and they were ordered to chant their death-songs if they dared. The Maqua immediately began in defiant tones to recount his own deeds of prowess on the war-path, and tell how many Hurons he had slain. He hurled defiance at his enemies, taunted them with their cowardice, and sought to so enrage them that they would kill him at once; but Nahma remained dumb. He had no deeds to tell of, nor was he in a humor to invent any.

Suddenly the Hurons made a rush at the one who thus defied them, and for a few minutes a fierce struggle raged about the helpless form. When next it appeared in view its scalp had been torn off, while the still living body was gashed and mutilated almost beyond recognition; but defiant words still issued chokingly from its trembling lips. The poor mortal frame was nearly spent, but its brave spirit was undaunted. The next act of torture was by fire. Blazing splinters of fat pine were thrust into the mangled body and hot ashes were poured on its bleeding head. Then a light was applied to the dry wood, and in another minute the eager flames were leaping high about their victim.

The awful tragedy was accompanied by shrieks of laughter, mocking yells, and a frantic dancing about the two young warriors, one of whom was thus made to serve as a hideous object lesson to the other. When the first was so nearly dead that his defiant utterances were reduced to mere gaspings for breath, the dancing demons turned their attention to the second victim, and prepared to inflict upon him a series of still more devilish torments.

Nahma had witnessed everything with fascinated gaze; but though sickened to the point of fainting, had made no movement nor uttered a sound to betray the agony of his thoughts. He now knew what to expect, and was nerving himself to endure to the end, as became a warrior. Aeana would never know, of course; but if by any chance the story of his last hour should reach her ear, she must have no excuse to call him "squaw."

One of his tormentors approached with a bar of iron heated until it glowed; for, through trading with the French, this metal was now known to the Indians of the St. Lawrence valley.

"Put out his eyes," shouted a spectator. "He has seen enough."

As the glowing iron approached his face Nahma instinctively closed his eyes; but a yell of derision from those near enough to note the movement caused him to open them again quickly. But even in that brief space something had happened, for the first thing on which they rested was a gigantic figure bounding towards him. It uttered inarticulate cries of rage and brandished a weapon. With a single blow from this it dashed to earth the man bearing the red-hot iron. Falling on his own instrument of torture, the wretch uttered a yell of pain as it seared his flesh. At the same moment the terrible new-comer levelled his weapon at the mutilated form bound to the opposite stake, and with a flash of lightning accompanied by a stunning burst of thunder, instantly freed the tortured spirit from its misery.

Before the smoke of the discharge cleared away the new-comer was beside Nahma, cutting savagely at his bonds. As the last one dropped he grasped the young warrior by an arm and led him a few paces from the cruel stake. Then turning to the sullen Hurons, who shrank from the indignant blaze of his eyes, he denounced them in bitter terms.

"You are worse than wolves," he cried. "You are scum and *canaille*. You are devils, and should be made to dwell forever in a pit of fire. Because you go forth to fight against a man and he meets you bravely, is that a reason for torturing him when the fortune of war has placed him helpless in your hands? This youth was the only one of all his people who dared attack me face to face and hand to hand. Better still, he was the only Iroquois brave enough to attempt the succor of their wounded chieftain. He is fleet of foot and might easily have escaped, but he would not go alone. So he fell into your inhuman hands, and as a reward for his bravery you propose to torture him to death. Bah! You make me so sick that I have a mind to sever all connection with you from this hour, and order my men to beat you from my sight with sticks. Now remember that this youth is *my* captive, and whoever touches so much as a hair of his head shall die, for I will not have him harmed.

"Come, lad, with me," added Champlain, turning to Nahma; "you shall eat and rest, and after that if you desire to return to your own people you shall be free to do so. Only it would please me to have you remain a little for instruction in the ways of white men and the making of a better acquaintance between us, for I have taken a fancy to you beyond any that I have yet entertained for a native of this wilderness."

Although Nahma understood no word of what the marvellous stranger said, he recognized the friendly tone and gesture, and was quite willing to follow wherever the other might lead. As they were about to move away a chief of the Hurons stood in the path and begged for a hearing.

"It is true," he said, "that we would have killed this young man; but it is because we thought our white father angry that he still lived. Also is it true that in any case we should have put him to death on reaching the place of our own people. We must have done this, for if we should let him live he would sooner or later make an escape, and in escaping would surely kill some of our people. It is because he is a brave warrior that we could not let him live to do us mischief. If he were a coward, then could we make of him a slave to hoe corn with the squaws; but with a brave man this might not be done. Also because of his bravery would we have tested him by fire, that he might give proof of his courage to the very end of his life. Any brave man, Huron or Iroquois, would rather perish at the stake than live the life of a slave. It is our way, and if it be not also the way of our white father, let him not cover us with shame on account of it, for we have not yet learned one that is better."

"You have spoken well," answered Champlain, "and already am I penitent for my hasty words, since, as you say, you were only acting according to your conception of what is right. Therefore I forgive you and will continue to extend the hand of friendship. At the same time, see you to it that no more atrocities are enacted in my presence. Also see to it that this youth is accorded the respect due him over whom my protection is extended."

So it came to pass that Nahma, son of Longfeather, now known as Massasoit the Iroquois, was saved from a dreadful death to become the companion of the first white man he had ever met, who was also one of the foremost adventurers of his age.

Although Champlain had laid aside his steel armor, he was still so utterly different in appearance from any person Nahma had ever seen that the latter continued to regard him as a supernatural being, and accompanied him with much trepidation. Also the youth was dazed by the peril he had just escaped and the strangeness of his deliverance.

As they went towards Champlain's own camp-fire, Nahma noticed for the first time that two more of the strange beings walked close beside them; and, listening to their conversation, though of course without understanding it, he all at once became convinced that they were indeed human like himself. Moreover, it flashed into his mind that they must be of that white race concerning which he had heard much talk in the lodge of Kaweras. By that shrewd Indian the apparently meaningless words repeated by Nahma during his illness had been conjectured to belong to the vocabulary of white men, and he had said as much to his young guest. Thinking of these things and acting upon a sudden impulse, just as they reached Champlain's separate camp Nahma exclaimed,—

"Hillo!"

The three white men stared at him in amazement.

"Sacré!" added the young warrior.

"What have we here?" cried Champlain. "A savage from the interior wilderness speaking both English and French. It is incredible.—My young friend, who taught you the tongues of the Old World? Where have you met white men?"

"Mass, I saw it," remarked Nahma. He was well pleased at the effect of the words already used, but looked for a still greater exhibition of amazement on the part of his hearers at this final utterance. To his disappointment, they only gazed blankly and evidently without understanding.

"That is evidently a native word, and must be his own name," said Champlain. "Massasoit. It hath a pleasing sound and fits well his aspect. Not only has he proved himself to be braver than any of his fellows, but he hath a look of superior intelligence. For these things I had thought to afford him opportunity of escaping during the night, and so of making his way back to his own people. Now, however, he has so aroused my interest and curiosity with his fluency in foreign tongues that I cannot afford to loose him until we are better acquainted. See to it, therefore, that he does not escape."

Thus Nahma, who if he had held his tongue would have been set free, was still retained as a captive and borne northward by the victorious Hurons. The journey down the lake, through the rapid Richelieu, and over the broad flood of the mighty St. Lawrence was full of interest and novel sensations to our lad. None of them was, however, to be compared with the wonder and amazement that filled his soul on the evening of the tenth day of travel, when they came to Quebec, and he gazed for the first time on the lodges of white men.

CHAPTER XIV

TWO INMATES OF A GUARD-HOUSE

Samuel de Champlain was one of the most daring and persistent of explorers in the New World. Before coming of age he visited the West Indies and Mexico, going down the Pacific coast of the latter country as far as Panama. Then as he crossed the isthmus he conceived the idea, which he afterwards made public, of a ship canal that should connect the two oceans. His next voyage, inspired by the published narrative of Jacques Cartier, carried him into the St. Lawrence and up that mighty river as far as Hochelaga (Montreal), which point Cartier had also reached nearly seventy years earlier.

Champlain subsequently explored the coasts of Canada and New England, helped to found the unfortunate settlements of St. Croix and Port Royal, and sailed to the southward as far as Cape Cod. On his way he stopped in Boston harbor, which he describes as being filled with heavily wooded islands. He also discovered the Charles River, and named it Rivière du Guast. On the following day he took refuge from a gale in Plymouth harbor, which he named Port St. Louis, and which he thus visited long before the Pilgrims landed on its shores.

After spending some years on the coast and crossing the Atlantic several times, the energetic Frenchman again entered the St. Lawrence and sailed as far as Stadaconie, where Cartier first and after him Roberval had planted ill-starred and short-lived settlements. At this point Champlain determined to establish a base from which to explore the vast regions that, hidden in savage mystery, stretched away indefinitely on all sides. It should also be head-quarters for the greatest fur trade the world had ever known, and for the religious institutions from which he hoped to spread Christianity among the heathen.

Here, then, on a narrow strand at the foot of towering cliffs, he set his men to work, and before the summer was ended they had erected three spacious buildings, enclosed them within a stout palisade, planted defensive batteries, dug a moat around the whole, cleared land for a garden, and opened up a trade with the neighboring Indians. Thus was begun a city destined to become one of the most important of the New World, and to it Champlain gave the name of Quebec, which was his pronunciation of a native word signifying a narrowing of the river.

In Quebec, twenty-seven years later, the great Frenchman died, leaving behind him a record of adventure and achievement such as but few others could show. He had succeeded where many had failed, and had established an empire in the New World. He had crossed the ocean more than a score of times to make himself equally welcome in the court circles of France and beside the council-fires of Huron warriors. He had explored the Ottawa to its head-waters, crossed the divide to Lake Nipissing, descended to Georgian Bay, and was the first white man to gaze upon the inland sea that he named Lake Huron. He next discovered Lake Ontario, crossed it in a bark canoe, and penetrated the Iroquois country as far as the site of Syracuse. In the beautiful lake that bears his name he has an enduring monument. He started on the journey that ended on Lake Champlain with the hope, then common to all explorers, of discovering a western passage to China, and only failed because he could not find what did not exist. Instead of it, he discovered, saved from an awful death, and carried to Quebec the youth who was to become known to the world as Massasoit, chief of the Wampanoags.

Champlain had long been looking for some young Indian of intelligence and proved courage whom he might teach to speak his own language, attach to his person, and employ to advantage in his proposed explorations. In Nahma he believed he had found all the desired qualities, and, what was still better, the youth, being an Iroquois, would never join any Huron conspiracy against the French. The shrewd adventurer was therefore greatly pleased with his prize and impatient to begin his training. At the same time he found his Huron allies so jealous of his liking for an Iroquois, that while he remained in their company he dared not treat his captive with any marked attention. He saw that Nahma was provided with food, and would not permit him to be beaten or abused, as were some of the prisoners, but that was all. He dared not even have the youth in his own canoe, much as he wished to gain his confidence. Thus, Nahma saw but little of his white companions on the weary journey that finally ended at Quebec.

At the mouth of the Richelieu the victorious war-party disbanded, the larger number, together with most of the prisoners, going up the St. Lawrence towards their homes on the Ottawa, and only half a dozen canoes of Montagnais, who dwelt on the Saguenay, followed Champlain down the great river. As these came within sight of Quebec they raised a triumphant war-song and plied their paddles with redoubled energy, while Champlain and the other white men discharged their muskets in token of victory. This was the first news of their absent leader received by the anxious garrison since his departure, and in their joy over his safe return they gave him a thunderous welcome from their cannon.

Not only did this dreadful sound nearly paralyze poor Nahma, but it so terrified a small party of Indians who were trading within the fort that they rushed from it in dismay, took to their canoes, and paddled off with all speed. So precipitate was their flight that they left behind one of their number, who in his terror had leaped from a second-story window of the trading house and broken a leg.

Champlain had left his infant colony in charge of Pierre Chauvin, a smart young officer, who now met him outside the palisades with tidings that caused an instant change of plan. The only ship that would return to France that year had dropped down to Tadousac for a lading of furs but two days earlier. For a moment Champlain hesitated, and then his mind was made up. He must board that ship before she sailed, for he had despatches of the utmost importance to send home by her. Thus he must immediately hasten to Tadousac. This decision he imparted to Chauvin, adding,—

"I will shortly return, and until then take thou good care of this youth." Here the speaker indicated Nahma. "See that he escape not, for his security is of importance to our cause. Keep him, then, safely until I come again, when I will inform thee further concerning him. *Au revoir, mon ami.* May the saints protect thee."

Thus saying, Champlain rejoined his Indian allies, who were impatient to be off, and in another minute was again sweeping down the great river. By his order Nahma had been hastily bundled ashore, and now stood gazing first at the wonderful structures rising close at hand and then at the disappearing canoes. Chauvin stood near by, biting his moustache and growling at his chief's sudden departure.

"I wish I were in his place," he muttered; "and if once I could set foot on shipboard I would sail away never again to revisit this detestable country. How now, you spawn! What are you staring at?" he cried, suddenly turning upon Nahma, who was looking curiously at him.

Chauvin hated Indians as he did everything else in the country that had so bitterly disappointed his dreams of easily acquired wealth, and he was disgusted that one of them should now be left in his care.

"Away with him to the guard-house!" he shouted to a couple of soldiers in attendance, "and keep him in close confinement until the governor's return, since that is his Excellency's order."

So Nahma was roughly hustled away, led inside the palisade, across the enclosed court, and thrust into the guard-house. It was a small structure solidly built of logs, having a rude stone chimney and a single unglazed window some eighteen inches square that was fitted with iron bars and could be closed from the outside by a heavy shutter. There were also bars across the throat of the chimney. The floor was of earth and the room was unfurnished. As the massive door of this dungeon swung to with a crash behind him the young Indian stood for a moment motionless. Then, in a frenzy of rage, he dashed himself against the immovable barrier, clutched at the window-bars in a vain effort to wrench them from their fastenings, and rushed about the narrow space, seeking some outlet, like a wild animal when first caged.

While our lad was thus engaged the door of his prison was again flung open and two soldiers entered. Still possessed by his frenzy, Nahma sprang forward, determined to kill them and make good his escape or die in the attempt; but the sight of a burden that they bore caused him to pause. It was the form of another Indian youth apparently helpless. Behind them came others bringing straw, two blankets, food, and a jug of water. With the straw and blankets they made a bed in one corner, on which they laid the wounded youth. Then without a word to the prisoner they departed, barring the door behind them.

Now our lad had at least something to occupy his mind and divert his thoughts from his own unhappiness. He saw that the new-comer was neither a Huron nor an Iroquois; but as he bent over him and began to ask questions he discovered that they had many words of the wide-spread Algonquin tongue in common. Thus he quickly learned that the other was named Tasquanto, that he was of a band of the Abenakis who had come to Quebec to trade, and that, terrified by the awful noise of cannon, he had leaped from a window and broken a leg. His comrades having deserted him, he had been brought to the guard-house that the only other Indian remaining in the fort might wait upon him.

So Nahma was provided with an occupation that probably prevented him from either killing himself in his despair or losing his mind. Thanks to the teaching of Kaweras, he was able to set and properly bandage Tasquanto's broken limb, and for weeks thereafter he was his fellow-prisoner's devoted attendant.

In the mean time the green of summer was succeeded by the gorgeous tints of autumn, and its short-lived glory gave way to the white desolation of a northern winter; but Champlain did not return to Quebec, nor did any word come from him. At the end of two months Chauvin sent messengers to Tadousac; but they returned without having seen a living soul, white or red; and not until the weary winter was half spent did the garrison of that lonely fort learn what had become of the leader whom they were mourning as dead.

CHAPTER XV

THE BITTER WINTER OF CANADA

The Canadian winter, that is now a time of so much animation and gayety in the city of Quebec, proved a season of terror, starvation, sickness, and death to the handful of Frenchmen left by Champlain to guard his infant settlement. At its beginning they recklessly squandered their stores, eating and drinking with no thought of the morrow. If Champlain had been with them he would have taught them differently, for he had already passed several winters in the country and knew their bitter meaning. But, lacking his wise guidance, they indulged in riotous living until suddenly they came face to face with famine. The winter was not more than half spent when this happened, and they began to suffer from hunger.

Now that it was too late for any real good, Chauvin seized every particle of food that remained, locked it up, and doled it out to his men in such meagre allowance as barely served to keep life in their shivering bodies. He also sent them into the woods to hunt, or to dig roots and groundnuts, with which to help out their scanty fare. He had expected to be able to purchase all the provisions he needed from Indians, who, during the summer, had brought game to the fort in abundance, but now not a native was to be seen except a few poor wretches who came empty-handed and as beggars.

Unlike their brethren of the south, who cultivated fields and stored harvests for the winter, the improvident dwellers of that region lived wholly by hunting, feasting while game was plentiful and starving when it was gone.

In all this time no one within the limits of that wretched fort suffered as did the son of Longfeather. From the day that he was thrust into his prison he was not allowed to leave it for a breath of outside air, or a glimpse of the freedom for which his soul longed, until it seemed as though he would rather die than remain within those hated walls another minute.

And with it all he had no idea why he was thus confined or what fate was in store for him. Only, as days, weeks, and months passed, he became more and more certain that he was to have no release save only by death itself. But one thing kept him from seeking this instead of waiting for it, and that was the friendship of the young Indian who, wounded and helpless, had been brought to him during the first hour of his imprisonment. Tasquanto's recovery was slow, and for many weeks he depended upon Nahma for everything.

It did not take long for these two, drawn to each other by the bonds of race and a common misfortune, to cement a friendship, and swear that they would either gain freedom or perish together.

Although they could not plan an escape from their closely guarded prison and must wait for chance to aid them, they spent hours in discussing the course to be pursued if ever they got beyond those hated walls.

"We must make all haste to cross the river," said Tasquanto, "for the Hurons would quickly kill us if we remained on this side. If it is frozen that will be easy. If not, we must steal one of the clumsy boats of these awkward white men, who make everything bigger and heavier than is needful. On the other side we will conceal ourselves until we can build a canoe, and then we will go southward. Beyond that I cannot see, for if we go to the country of thy people, they will kill me; while it would be dangerous for thee, an Iroquois, to be found in my country."

"But I am not of the Iroquois," protested Nahma.

"Not of the Iroquois! Who, then, are thy people?"

"That I know not. I was found among the Maquas, who are a tribe of the Iroquois, sorely wounded and without memory of aught that had ever happened before that time. Since then I have been an Iroquois by adoption, but it is certain that I am not one by birth."

This statement so changed the aspect of affairs that it was agreed they should travel towards the country of the Abenakis in case an escape could be effected. It also afforded a fruitful topic of speculation, and thus helped pass the weary hours.

Finally, the time came when Tasquanto was so fully recovered that he was sent out to hunt food for the hungry garrison, and during the day Nahma was left alone, since only at night was his companion allowed to rejoin him. Chauvin realized that if both were sent into the woods they would at once make good their escape; while, from the friendship he had noted between them, he felt assured that Tasquanto would return to his comrade so long as the latter was held. Nor did he dare allow Nahma to escape while there was a chance of Champlain's return.

So our poor lad shivered and starved in his hated prison-house, finding his only occupation in making snow-shoes from materials furnished by Tasquanto. He designed them for his own use, but they were taken from him by his guards as fast as completed, so that in the end he had nothing to show for his labors. One night a great grief befell him; Tasquanto failed to appear at the usual hour, nor did he come during the night, though Nahma watched and waited for him until morning. He asked eager questions of the guard who brought his miserable breakfast, but the man refused to answer, and all that day our lad sat in a lethargy of despair, careless whether he lived or died.

The following night was one of furious storm and bitter cold. The north wind roaring through the bending forest shrieked and howled in savage glee as it struck the forlorn little outpost of white men. It leaped down the wide-throated chimneys and scattered their fires. It slammed shutters and doors, while if any ventured abroad, it blinded and choked them with stinging volleys of snowdrift. So fierce and deadly was it that even military discipline came to an end, and all sentries were permitted to abandon their posts.

Nahma sat alone in the dark, numbed and nearly perished with the cold, for he had burned up the last bit of fuel brought him two days earlier by Tasquanto, and none had been supplied since. In the many voices of the storm, now shrill and clamorous, then deep and menacing, and again filled with weird moanings that died in long-drawn sighs, he heard the spirits of the dead, the Okis of another world, calling to him, and bidding him share their wild freedom. He knew that he had but to yield to the drowsiness already overpowering him, and the deadly cold would speedily release him from all earthly prisons. Perhaps Tasquanto's spirit was among those now calling; yes, he was sure of it, for he recognized his friend's voice. "Massasoit," it called, "Massasoit, wake up! It is I, Tasquanto, thy brother. Wake up and come to me."

The cry was agonized in its intensity, and after a little even Nahma's dulling senses recognized that it was uttered by human lips. At the same time he felt that the storm was beating on his face, and struggling weakly to his feet, he gained the window through which it came. Its shutter was wide open, and beyond its bars stood Tasquanto speaking to him.

"I thought thee dead, my brother, for I have called many times without answer," said Tasquanto, as he became aware that his friend was at hand.

"And I believed thy voice to be that of thy spirit, for I also thought thee gone to the place of the dead," replied Nahma. "Why have you remained away from me these many hours?"

"It is because they drove me from the gate, saying that my hunting was of no avail, and that I should not longer eat of their stores. But I could not go, my brother, without word with thee, and now has the storm-god given me a chance for speaking. If it were not for these bars we could do more than speak, for those who kept guard have been driven to shelter, and there is none to hinder us from going away together. But they may not be broken, and so we must wait until other means are found for thy release. But fear not that I will desert thee. I have found a way for passing the wall, and will come to this place whenever it may be done without notice. In the mean time I will prepare for our flight. Already have I built a lodge in a safe place beyond the river, and——"

Here Tasquanto's words were suddenly interrupted, and the heavy shutter was slammed to as though by a fierce gust of wind. Then the door was flung open and the faint gleam of a horn lantern illumined the interior.

A little earlier on that same evening Chauvin, while talking with one of his officers concerning Champlain and his unexplained absence, had been reminded of the young Indian whom the governor had consigned to his care, but to whom he had not given a thought in many days. Now he inquired carelessly whether he were alive or dead.

"I know not," replied the officer, who, following his chief's example, had not concerned himself about the fate of so insignificant a being as a captive Indian.

"And why do you not know?" cried Chauvin, with a sudden burst of petulant rage. "It is your duty to know, and to be ready with instant report concerning everything taking place within the walls of Quebec. Do you think because the governor chooses to absent himself for a while that no one is left here to maintain his authority? By the saints, monsieur, I will give you cause to remember that Pierre Chauvin is not to be trifled with, and that when he asks a question he expects it to be promptly answered. Go, then, at once, sir, and inform yourself by personal observation of the condition of this prisoner, or haply you may find yourself in his place."

Without daring to reply, the bewildered officer bowed and left the room. Thus it happened that, accompanied by a soldier whom he had summoned to attend him, he came to Nahma's prison-house in time to interrupt the conversation between him and Tasquanto and frighten the latter into a precipitate retreat.

Finding, to his satisfaction, that the prisoner was still alive, the officer demanded of the soldier why, in such weather, he was kept without fire.

The soldier replied that it had been left to the other Indian to provide the guard-house with fuel; whereupon his superior passed out to him the rating he himself had received from Chauvin.

"And so, *canaille*, you leave your duties to be performed by a miserable skulking savage. A pretty state of affairs in a king's fortress. Bring wood at once, sir, and fire, also fetch something in the way of food, for this wretch looks like to die of starvation, a thing that may not be allowed of the governor's own prisoner, even though he be a heathen."

So on that night of bitter tempest not only were Nahma's spirits raised by a new hope, but the horrors of freezing and starvation that had threatened his life were sensibly mitigated. Two days later came the first word received from Champlain since his hurried departure for Tadousac four months earlier.

CHAPTER XVI

A DASH FOR LIBERTY

The mystery of Champlain's disappearance weighed heavily on the spirits of the forlorn little garrison left to hold Quebec. He had been the life and mainstay of the colony, the firm rock upon which it was founded. Without him there seemed no hope of its continuance or of relief from their distress. They were convinced that he was dead, for they knew he would never have left them without at least sending a message to tell where he had gone. So they mourned him sincerely if also selfishly, and planned to abandon his settlement at the first opportunity, if indeed any should offer.

The great storm cast an added gloom over the garrison, and they were so unhappy that every man was ready to fly at his neighbor's throat upon the slightest provocation, when a small band of Indians was reported to be making a camp near at hand. Instantly every face brightened, for it was thought that they must have brought provisions to trade for goods. Thus, when, a little later, one of them approached the fort, he was given prompt admittance. Being conducted to the presence of the commandant, he announced that his people were so very hungry that they had come to the white men to beg a little food from their abundant stores. At the same time he had brought a message from the great white chief, for which he was entitled to a reward.

With this the Indian produced a folded paper, greasy and grimed with dirt, which he handed to Chauvin.

As the latter unfolded it he uttered an exclamation, for it contained a note written in French and signed "Champlain." Its condition rendered it difficult to decipher, but as the reader gradually mastered its contents his face darkened, until suddenly he sprang up, seized a stick, and began furiously to belabor the astonished savage, who had been waiting in smiling expectancy for his reward. With a howl of pained surprise, he leaped back and rushed from the building with the enraged commandant in hot pursuit.

Not until the terrified native had escaped from the fort and disappeared in the forest did Chauvin give over his chase. Then, to the amazement of his men, he ordered a cannon to be loaded and fired in the direction taken by the object of his wrath. Although the crashing ball did no damage, it, and the roar of the gun bursting upon the winter stillness, so frightened the recently arrived Indians that they instantly abandoned their partially constructed camp and fled in hot haste from that hostile neighborhood.

Refusing to answer questions, and so leaving the curiosity of his men unsatisfied, Chauvin returned to his quarters, and lifting Champlain's note from the floor where he had flung it, read it for the second time with gritting teeth and bitter maledictions. It was dated four months earlier, and read as follows:

My Good Friend Pierre:

I am just arrived at Tadousac and find the ship about to sail. I also find it to be of the last importance that one of us should return in her to France. Had I known this two days earlier, or could I get word to you in season, the mission would devolve upon you, since I am loath to leave at this time. As it happens, I myself must go; but will return in earliest spring. So, my friend, until then everything is left to you. Husband carefully your provisions, keep up the spirits of your men, and maintain friendly relations with the natives. I forward this by a messenger, whom you will suitably reward for its prompt delivery. Regretting that we may not exchange duties, for I would gladly remain, I sign myself, as ever,

Thy friend,

Champlain.

"Death and furies!" cried Chauvin, again flinging the note to the floor and grinding it beneath his heel. "To think that while we have mourned him as dead he has been all the time comfortably in France. Also that I might have gone in his stead if only he could have got word to me in time. Ten thousand thunders! It would enrage a saint! Maintain friendly relations with the natives, forsooth! I would I could blow them all to eternity. Suitably reward that rascal messenger! Burning at the stake would be too good for him. And, heavens! all this time we have been keeping one of the scoundrels in luxurious idleness, gorging him with food robbed from our own bellies, providing him with fire and lodging to gratify a whim of the governor's, doubtless long since forgotten. But not another minute shall he thus impose upon us. He shall go, and that with such speed as will amaze him."

With this the angry commandant again descended to the court, summoned all the able-bodied men of the garrison, and bade them form a double line outside the guard-house door, after first providing themselves with cudgels. "The red whelp inside," he said, "has without recompense devoured our substance long enough. Now, therefore, I propose to send him forth bearing tokens of our regard that may not be forgotten in haste. Watch sharply, then, and remember that any man failing to deal him at least one blow shall go without his supper this night. Are you ready? It is well!"

Thus saying, Chauvin unlocked the guard-house door and flung it open preparatory to stepping inside and driving out with blows its solitary occupant. The next moment he was hurled sprawling to the ground, and a slight, half-naked figure, animated by desperation, was darting with such speed between the lines of unprepared soldiers that some failed even to go through the motions of striking at him, while others wasted their blows on the empty air. Uttering yells of delight at the novel nature of this entertainment, they ran after him; but they might as well have pursued a fleeting shadow. Before they could head him off he had sped through the open gate and was gone.

After Tasquanto's visit Nahma's shutter had been nailed up, so that he no longer had even the poor consolation of gazing out on the blank wall of palisades. Nor could he employ his hands, for he was now in darkness, save for such faint gleams as filtered down his chimney. Under these conditions he believed that he might speedily die, and planned for one last effort at escape before his waning strength should turn to utter weakness. On that very day he had determined that when next his prison door was opened it should never again close on his living body. So he sat watching it with feverish impatience.

The roar of Chauvin's vengeful cannon startled him and at the same time gave him a vague hope of some unusual happening that might result in his favor. So he became keenly alert, and was not taken by surprise when, without previous warning, the door of the guard-house was flung open. Dropping from his shoulders the blanket which alone had saved him from freezing, the youth sprang forward, reckless of consequences, and a minute later, without an idea of how the miracle had been accomplished, found himself outside the fort and speeding towards the icebound river. So blinded were his eyes by the unaccustomed light and glare of snow that until now he had seen nothing save the figure that had opened his door, and his movements had been guided by instinct rather than knowledge. The single fact indelibly impressed upon his brain was that Tasquanto waited somewhere beyond the river. Consequently that was the one direction for him to take, and he would doubtless have plunged into its waters, had they been free, as readily as he now leaped upon its snow-covered surface.

So long as he was within sight of the fort and within range of its guns his strength lasted, and he sped forward with the same fleetness that had formerly aroused the wonder of his Iroquois friends. Thus he gained the middle of the river, and climbed a rugged ridge of hummocks and huge ice-blocks upheaved during the final struggle of rebellious waters against the mighty forces of the frost-king.

On the farther side of this our poor lad faltered, staggered, and then sank with a groan. The nervous strength that had borne him thus far was exhausted, and in this place of temporary safety it yielded to the weakness of his long imprisonment. He had made a splendid dash for liberty, but now he had reached the limit of his powers, and must either be recaptured within a short space or die of the bitter cold. Even as he lay with closed eyes gasping for breath he felt its numbing clutch, and knew that very shortly he would be powerless against it. But it did not matter. He would at least die in possession of the freedom for which he had longed, and, after all, what had he to live for? He was friendless, homeless, and without even a people whom he might call his own. No tribe claimed him, there was no lodge within which he had the right of shelter. It would be much better in the land of spirits, for there his own would know him as he would know them. The trail to it was easy and short, also it was a very pleasant path, bright with sunshine and gay with flowers. There was music of singing birds, and already were the voices of his own people calling to him. "Massasoit!" they cried, "Massasoit!" Then they named him brother and bade him open his eyes that he might see them. So he opened his eyes and gazed into the anxious face of Tasquanto, who knelt beside him rubbing vigorously at his limbs and slapping him smartly to restore circulation in the numbing body.

He smiled happily at sight of Nahma's unclosed eyes, but did not for an instant desist from his rubbings and slappings until the other at length sat up, and then unsteadily regained his feet.

"Now, my brother," said Tasquanto, taking a robe of skins from his own shoulders as he spoke and throwing it about Nahma, "together must we reach the lodge I have prepared, for I will never return to it alone. The trail is long and hard, but it must be overcome or we shall perish together."

So the journey was begun, Nahma at first leaning heavily on his comrade's supporting arm, but gaining new strength with each step. As he had taken neither nourishment nor stimulant, this was wholly owing to the effect upon his spirits of renewed hope and a cheery companionship. As they walked Tasquanto told him how, ever since the storm, his attempts at communication had been frustrated, how in the mean time he had increased the comforts of his hidden lodge, how at sound of Chauvin's cannon he had hastened towards the fort to learn the cause of the firing, and of the overwhelming joy with which he had discovered Nahma as the latter topped the ice-ridge in the middle of the river. Then Nahma related as well as he could the details of his wonderful escape from the fort, and by the time his narrative was ended they were come to the rude lodge that Tasquanto had built in anticipation of just such a need as had now arisen.

CHAPTER XVII

A DEATH-DEALING THUNDER-STICK

Tasquanto's lodge was snugly hidden in a dense growth of heavy timber near the place where the Chaudière flows into the St. Lawrence. It was merely a frame of poles covered so thickly with branches of fragrant spruce and balsam that it presented the appearance of a green mound rising above the surrounding snow. Its walls were so thick as to be almost wind-proof, and in the middle of its earthen floor was a small circle of stones that formed a rude fireplace. In this only the dryest of wood was burned, and the little smoke that resulted escaped through an aperture left in the roof. On two sides were elastic beds of spruce boughs covered deep with flat hemlock branches and balsam tips. The very air of the place was a tonic, and the escaped captive, fresh from the foulness of his prison, drew in eager breaths of its life-giving sweetness as he sank wearily, but happily, down on the nearest pile of boughs.

As he lay there gazing about the rude shelter with an air of perfect content he uttered frequent exclamations of amazement, for Tasquanto was drawing from various hiding-places an array of treasures such as no Indian of Nahma's acquaintance had ever before possessed: a copper kettle, a steel hatchet, two knives, a blanket, several glass bottles, and a fragment of mirror. Then, with conscious pride, but also with evident trepidation, he produced the most wonderful trophy of all, a rusty musket, one of the awful thunder-sticks that rendered the white man all-powerful.

During the night of the great storm the entire garrison of Quebec had gathered for warmth in the hall of the commandant's house, and Tasquanto had taken advantage of this to make a foray into the deserted barracks with the above result. He had brought away the musket with fear and trembling, dreading lest it might explode and kill him at any moment. Even now he handled it cautiously, while Nahma could not for some time be persuaded to touch it. So it was laid carefully down, and he was permitted to feast his eyes on the marvel while Tasquanto busied himself in preparing a feast of more substantial character.

He had been so fortunate as to discover the winter den of a bear, which he had also succeeded in killing, so that now he could offer his guest not only the warmth of a shaggy robe but an abundance of meat. Instead of half-burning and half-cooking a chunk of this on the coals, as was the custom of his people, he displayed a rudiment of civilization by cutting it up into small bits and stewing them in his copper kettle.

After the youths had eaten heartily of this meal, which, simple as it was, proved more satisfactory to Nahma than the very best of those given him in Quebec, they spent several hours in discussing their plans for the future and in examining Tasquanto's treasures. Having overcome his awe of the thunder-stick sufficiently to take it in his hands, Nahma became anxious to test its powers. He had seen Champlain discharge his musket, and knew that it was done through the agency of a lighted slow-match applied to the priming-pan. His knowledge of the firing of a gun was thus far in advance of Tasquanto's, who, having never witnessed the operation at close range, had no idea of how it was accomplished. But he was quite willing to learn, and so it was agreed that on the following morning Nahma should give the owner of the musket his first lesson in its use.

Both of them were so excited over the prospect of experimenting for their own benefit with the deadly thunder of the white man that they lay awake most of the night discussing their proposed adventure; and, as a consequence, slept much later than they had intended on the following morning. The day was well advanced, therefore, when the two lads, after preparing and eating another hearty meal, stepped outside to test their newly acquired weapon. It was carried by Nahma, who, nervous with excitement, still presented a bold front, while, under his direction, Tasquanto fetched a blazing brand from the fire.

Resting the barrel of his piece across the trunk of a prostrate tree and holding its stock at arm's length, Nahma bade his companion apply fire to the pan. With much trepidation and a strong desire to clap both hands to his ears, Tasquanto valiantly did as he was bidden, but without result. Again and again did he apply the glowing coal, but still the gun refused to obey the wishes of its inexperienced owners.

"It will only speak and deal out its death-medicine at the command of white men," said Tasquanto, disconsolately.

"Not so," replied Nahma, "for once I saw it obey the will of a Huron warrior. But I think I know what is needed. It must be turned over so that the flame may rise to it. Also in this weather the thunder-stick is so cold that it will take much fire to warm it into action. Make, therefore, a hot blaze, and I am assured that something will happen."

So Nahma turned the gun, and, forgetting to remain at arm's length, bent anxiously over the refractory piece, while Tasquanto built a regular fire beneath it. Of a sudden the musket went off with a tremendous report that roused the woodland echoes for miles. Also it sprang savagely backward, bowling over both Nahma and Tasquanto as though they had been ninepins.

But the most astounding result of the discharge was a series of shrieks and yells that resounded through the forest as though it were peopled by a pack of demons. At the same time a number of leaping figures dashed from an extensive thicket at which the gun had been inadvertently pointed and fled as though for their lives. Something had assuredly happened.

As our bewildered lads cautiously lifted their heads to learn the extent of the damage done by the fearful force they had so recklessly let loose, each was thankful to see that the other was still alive. Next they glanced at the musket. It lay half buried in the snow, looking as innocent and harmless as a stick of wood; but they knew of what terrible things it was capable, and would hereafter be very careful how they allowed it to come into contact with fire. They were convinced that in some unexplained manner it could absorb flame until it had accumulated a certain quantity and could then eject this with deadly effect.

Being reassured concerning their own condition and the present harmlessness of the musket, they next bethought themselves of the dreadful cries that had seemed to mingle with the report, and they agreed that these must have been uttered by the Okis, or spirits of the forest, in protest against such a rude disturbance of its winter quiet. As they stiffly picked themselves up, Nahma declared his intention of visiting the thicket towards which the thunder-stick had been pointed, to see whether he could discover where its lightnings had struck. Tasquanto tried to dissuade him, declaring that the place must be the abode of Okis; but to this Nahma answered that if so they were certainly frightened away for the present, which would therefore be the best time to visit their haunts.

So the two cautiously made their way in that direction, and had not gone more than fifty paces when they came upon a sight almost as startling as had been the discharge of the musket. It was the dead body of a Huron warrior not yet cold. His life's blood still trickled from a jagged wound in the breast and crimsoned the snow on which he had fallen. On all sides of him were other signs that told as plainly as spoken words how narrowly our lads had escaped falling into the hands of a merciless foe. There were marks of a cautious approach along the trail they themselves had made the day before, of the halt for observation when the intended victims were discovered, and of the panic-stricken flight that followed the unexpected musket-fire by which one of their number had been so suddenly killed.

"The thunder-stick is indeed a god," remarked Nahma. "It can discover and kill the enemies of those to whom it is friendly even before they have knowledge of approaching danger."

"Yes," replied Tasquanto, as he coolly scalped the dead Huron; "with it to fight on our side we are become as sagamores, terrible and all-powerful. I will take it to my own people, and when it shall lead them in battle who will be able to stand before them? Even the white men, whom many still think to be gods, are now no stronger than we. Oh, my friend! let us shout for joy, since in all the world there is no man more powerful than are Massasoit and Tasquanto, his brother."

When the exultant young warriors returned to camp, bearing with them the trophies of their exploit, they also carried, very reverently, the weapon which they termed a "thunder-god," and which had rendered them such notable service. Then, while Nahma set to work on a pair of snow-shoes, Tasquanto, who had seen the French soldiers oil and burnish their guns, coated his with bear's grease, removed its smoke-stains, and rubbed its barrel until it shone. When he had done for it everything that his limited knowledge prescribed, he placed it in a corner where they could constantly admire it, and began the construction of a rude toboggan of bark.

By the time this was completed Nahma's snow-shoes were also ready for service, and the fugitives were prepared to start on their long southward journey. For a beginning of this they made their way slowly up to the headwaters of the Chaudière, crossed a rugged divide to those of the Penobscot, and there established a permanent camp. From this they set lines of traps that yielded a rich reward in the way of pelts, and before spring opened they got out the frame of a canoe. As soon as sap began to run in the birch-trees they secured enough bark to cover it, and by the time the river opened they were prepared to float with its current to the country of Tasquanto's people.

Their voyage down the swift-rushing river was filled with adventures and with hair-breadth escapes. Not only were they in almost constant danger from foaming rapids and roaring waterfalls, but only unceasing vigilance and an occasional display of their musket saved them from death or capture by the hostile tribes through whose territory they passed.

At length they carried around the last cataract and entered upon the long, broad reaches by which the river flowed in dignified majesty to the sea. This was Tasquanto's country, and now they might watch for the villages in which he would be assured a friendly welcome.

Finally one was sighted, and Nahma proposed that, after the custom of white men on returning from victorious expeditions, they should discharge their thunder-stick. Nothing loath to add to his own importance by such an announcement of their coming, Tasquanto promptly assented to this proposition. So they landed a few hundred yards above the village and made preparations for the second discharge of their formidable weapon.

CHAPTER XVIII

KIDNAPPED

Being by this time, as they fondly imagined, thoroughly acquainted with the white man's thunder-stick and with all details of the process necessary to render it effective, our young Indians were determined to leave undone nothing that might contribute to the complete success of their proposed salute. To begin with, the musket must be pointed away from the village, and they themselves must keep at a respectful distance while it was accumulating its fiery energy. Also, to produce an extraordinary volume of sound, the flame by which the thunder-stick was fed must be big and hot. They knew this, because on the occasion of their previous experiment they had, with the aid of a flame, produced a much louder noise than that made by the white man's slow-matches. Consequently they argued that the greater the flame the louder the report.

At the same time they were willing to acknowledge that slow-matches were excellent things to have under certain conditions, when, for instance, one was so closely beset that he wished to fire with great rapidity, even as many as two or three shots in the course of an hour. So they were determined to obtain one at the very first opportunity, and imagined that thus provided their shooting equipment would be complete.

But a blaze would be much better for their present purpose, and they would take care that it was big enough to produce an astonishing result. So carefully did they make their preparations that while Tasquanto collected dry wood for the fire, Nahma cut a couple of forked sticks on which to rest the musket and drove them solidly into the ground. To these he lashed the gun until it resembled a victim about to be burned at the stake. He did not, of course, forget to place it upside down, so that its firing-pan might receive full benefit of the upleaping flames. Then wood was piled beneath it until it really looked as though they were intent upon burning the gun instead of being merely desirous of discharging it.

While they were making these preparations several of the villagers, noticing the presence of strangers, came out to discover their business. To these Tasquanto made the peace sign, and at the same time warned them not to come too close. So they halted and watched with curiosity the mysterious proceedings of the strangers.

At length all was in readiness, and Tasquanto, as principal owner of the thunder-stick, claimed the privilege of setting fire to the inflammable structure he had reared beneath it. As the brisk blaze shot upward he ran back and joined Nahma at a safe distance. On the opposite side were the village Indians, filled with uneasy expectancy mingled with awe; for they imagined they were witnessing some impressive religious ceremony.

The flames mounted higher and higher until they completely enveloped the devoted musket, and Tasquanto, so excited as to be unconscious of the act, clapped his hands to his ears to deaden the sound of the thunderous report that he momentarily expected. But it did not come. The wooden stock of the gun began to smoke, and then burst into a blaze. Being very dry and also saturated with oil, it was speedily consumed. At the same time the lashings burned through, and the red-hot barrel, already bent out of shape, fell into the glowing coals.

As though drawn by an irresistible fascination, Tasquanto, with hands still held to his ears, had moved nearer step by step, gazing with incredulous eyes at this destruction of the thing he had regarded as a god, loud-voiced and invincible. The puzzled spectators on the other side also cautiously approached closer.

Suddenly Tasquanto, seeming to awake as from a dream, started down the hill-side towards the canoe, and Nahma followed him. Both knew why they fled. For some unexplained reason their expected triumph had resulted in a dismal failure. This had laid them open to the ridicule that an Indian finds especially hard to bear, and they had no wish to be questioned concerning what had just taken place.

The spectators of their recent remarkable performance, curious to see what they would do next, followed them so closely that, in order to escape, our lads were forced to run. Gaining their canoe, they shoved it off and leaped in as the foremost of their pursuers reached the water's edge. Without heeding the many invitations to return that quickly became threatening commands, Nahma and Tasquanto plied their paddles with such diligence that they were quickly beyond arrow range; and, speeding past the village without a pause, they were soon lost to sight of its puzzled inhabitants. Not until they were some miles farther down the river was a word exchanged between the young men. Then, as Nahma drew in his paddle and paused for breath, he remarked,—

"The thunder-stick of the white man is bad medicine for bow-and-arrow people."

"Yes," replied Tasquanto, mournfully, "it seems that we have much to learn."

While in camp that night discussing the humiliating events of the day they were joined by a solitary hunter who was on his way up the river. After a guarded interchange of questions and answers, during which neither party learned anything definite concerning the other, the stranger told them of certain white men who were trading at the mouth of the Penobscot, and advised them to carry their furs to that market.

"Are they Française?" asked Nahma, who was determined never again to fall within the power of those who had so cruelly imprisoned him.

"No," was the reply, "they are of a people who call themselves 'Yengeese' and who make war on the white-coats."

"Have they thunder-sticks?" asked Tasquanto.

"In plenty."

"Then let us go to them. If we accomplish nothing else we may learn the white man's secret, and so shall our shame be wiped out."

On the following day, therefore, a few hours carried our lads to where the river broadened into a bay dotted with islands. As their little craft was lifted on the first great swells that came rolling in from the open sea, Nahma uttered an exclamation and pointed eagerly.

"Look!" he cried. "What is it? Was ever such a thing seen in the world before?"

Tasquanto glanced in the direction indicated and laughed. Truly, the sight was remarkable, and one still rare to those waters; but he had already seen one so similar in the St. Lawrence that he could now speak with the authority of superior knowledge.

"It is the winged canoe of the white man," he said. "In it he comes up out of the great salt waters and after a little flies back again to his own place. Knew you not that his whiteness is caused by the washing of the waters in which he lives?"

"No," replied Nahma, doubtfully. "Nor did I know that any canoe could be so vast. It even has trees growing from it."

"Yes," admitted the other, to whom this phenomenon was also a puzzle. "But they be not trees that bear fruit, nor even leaves, though they have branches and vines. On them the canoe spreads its wings, which are white like the pinions of wembezee" (the swan).

"Let us go closer that we may see these things," said Nahma, to whom the appearance of that little English trading-ship was as wonderful as had been his first view of Quebec.

So they approached slowly and cautiously, feasting their eyes on the marvel as they went, and directing each other's attention to a myriad of details. Finally they were within hailing distance, and a man standing on the ship's towering poop-deck beckoned for them to come on board.

Tasquanto, who knew the etiquette of such occasions, held up a beaver-skin, as much as to say "Will you trade?"

For reply the white man displayed some trinkets that glittered in the sunlight, thereby intimating his willingness to transact business. At the same time he turned to one who stood close at hand and said,—

"They be two young bucks, without old men, women, or children. Nor is there another native in sight. It is therefore the best chance by far that has offered for filling Sir Ferdinando's order. 'Twenty pounds will I give thee, Dermer, for a native youth of intelligence delivered here at Plymouth in good condition.' Those were his very words, and it will be well to have two; for if one dies on the passage, as the cattle are so apt to do, then will the other make good the loss. If both survive, so much the better, since we can readily dispose of the extra one. We must entice them on board, therefore, and the instant they set foot on deck do thou see to it that they are secured. Be careful, however, that they suffer no injury, for I would get them across in good condition if possible."

"Aye, aye, sir," answered the other, who was mate of the ship. "If you can toll 'em on board I'll handle them as they were unweaned lambs. I'll warrant you they won't escape if once I get a grip on them, slippery devils though they be."

When the canoe ran alongside the ship a few trinkets were tossed into it as presents and in token of good-will. Then a ladder of rope was lowered, and by signs our lads were invited to come on board.

They looked at each other doubtfully. "Is it safe to trust these white men?" asked Nahma.

"To discover the secret of the thunder-sticks, and perhaps to obtain one in exchange for our furs, is worth a risk," replied Tasquanto. As he spoke he glanced longingly up to where the ship's captain, with a leer on his face that passed for a reassuring smile, tempted them by a lavish display of trade goods.

"Truly, it would be worth much," hesitated Nahma. "At the same time, having once escaped from a prison, I have no desire to see the inside of another."

"Then stay thou here while I go," said Tasquanto, whose desire to wipe out his recent humiliation was so great as to overcome his prudence. "The secret of the thunder-stick I must have even though it cost me my life."

"Does my brother think so meanly of me as to believe that I would let him face a danger alone while I remained in safety?" inquired Nahma, reproachfully. "Let him go and I will follow close at his heels; for whatever happens to one of us must happen to both."

So the canoe was made fast, the bundle of furs was attached to a line let down for it, and Tasquanto began to climb the swaying ladder while Nahma steadied it from below. As the former disappeared over the ship's side the son of Longfeather followed swiftly after him. Topping the high bulwarks, he glanced anxiously down in search of his comrade, but Tasquanto was not to be seen. A suspicion of foul play darted into his mind, but too late for him to act upon it, for at the same instant he was seized by two pair of brawny hands and dragged inboard.

Half an hour later the ship under full canvas was speeding merrily down the bay with her jubilant crew bawling out the chorus of a homeward-bound chantey.

CHAPTER XIX

SOLD AS A SLAVE

The distress and terror of our poor lads when they found themselves flung into the horrible darkness of the ship's hold with its hatch closed above them would have been pitiful had there been any witnesses. But there was none, and for many weary hours they seemed to have been imprisoned in mere wantonness only to be forgotten as soon as the treacherous act had been accomplished. Their sole comfort was that they were together; for, on being dropped into the hold, Nahma found Tasquanto, stunned by the magnitude of his misfortune, awaiting him.

For a time the two remained speechless, only holding to each other, listening, and fearfully awaiting what next might happen. Although they could see nothing there was much to hear, for the anchor was being hove up, sails loosed and sheeted home, canvas was slatting, yards were creaking, and all to the accompaniment of much hoarse shouting and a continual tramping of heavy feet. But none of these sounds conveyed to our captives the slightest idea of what was taking place. After a while the ship began to heel until they believed her to be capsizing, and that their last hour had come. Also they heard a sound of rushing waters. A little later both were so utterly prostrated by sea-sickness that whatever might happen no longer concerned them.

In this wretched plight they lay for what seemed like many days, but in reality only until the middle of the next forenoon, when, of a sudden, the hatch above them was removed and they were blinded by the flood of light that followed. Then men came to them and they were driven on deck, where, dazed and weak with illness, they staggered from side to side with the motion of the ship. Their pitiable appearance was greeted by shouts of coarse mirth from the crew, who found in it a vastly entertaining spectacle.

The captives were offered food, but refused it with loathing, though they drank eagerly from a bucket of water placed beside them as they sat on deck at the foremast's foot. After a while Nahma became sufficiently revived by the fresh air to gaze about him with somewhat of interest in his strange surroundings. Everything was marvellous and incomprehensible. Even the bearded sailors in petticoats and pigtails, which latter he took to be scalp-locks, were entirely different from the French, who, until now, were the only white men he had known. Nor could he comprehend a word of the barbarous language in which they conversed. When he was tired of looking at them he began to wonder in which direction lay the land, and to turn over in his mind a plan for making a quick rush to the ship's side, leaping overboard, and swimming to shore.

Before broaching this scheme to his comrade Nahma decided to get his bearings. So he gained his feet and mounted a scuttle-butt, by which his eyes were lifted above the level of the high bulwarks. To his consternation there was no land in sight. Not so much as a tree nor a blue hill-top could he discover in any direction. His unaccustomed eyes could not even distinguish the line of the horizon dividing a gray sky from the immensity of gray waters that stretched away on all sides. The bewildering sight filled him with a dread greater than any he had ever known, and he slipped back to his place beside Tasquanto, utterly hopeless.

"Whether we be going up or down I know not," he said to the latter; "but certain it is that we now float among the clouds, with no prospect of ever again returning to the earth on which dwell people after our own kind. Already are we become Okis."

"Then is it a most unhappy condition," answered Tasquanto, "and the medicine-men are liars."

After a few hours on deck our lads were again driven into the darkness and foulness of the hold; but on every pleasant day thereafter for weeks was the process of bringing them on deck for an airing repeated. In times of storm they were kept below, with their sufferings immeasurably increased by sickness, by the violent pitching of the ship, by lack of food and water, and by terrors of the creakings and groanings that filled the surrounding blackness.

For more than a month did they thus suffer, hopeless of ever again sighting land or of any relief from their unhappy situation. Then, to Nahma at least, came the worst of all. One day, while they were on deck, he suddenly lifted his head and sniffed the air.

"It is a breath of earth," he whispered, as though fearful of uttering the glad news aloud. "I can smell it. Oh, my brother! to once more gain the freedom of a forest would be a happiness exceeding any other. Let us be ready on the morrow when we are again brought into the light. It may be that we shall be near enough to swim to the land. Once within cover of the forest we would never again look upon the face of a white man."

About this time they were sent below, but that faint scent of land not yet distinguished by any other on the ship had infused them with a new hope, and for hours they talked of what might be done on the morrow.

In the mean time their ship was so near the English coast that twenty-four hours later she lay at anchor in the harbor of Plymouth and her small boat was ready to go ashore.

"Fetch me the heathen desired by Sir Ferdinando," ordered Captain Dermer.

"Which one, sir?"

"Either will do. Call them up and take the first that shows a head. Drive the other back, and keep him below until my return."

"Aye, aye, sir."

So the hatch was partially removed, and the signal for which our lads had waited so impatiently was given. Tasquanto was first to answer it and gain the deck. Nahma followed closely, but was met by a blow that tumbled him back into the hold. Then the hatch was replaced, and he was once more confronted by the horrors of solitary confinement.

For a time he continued to hope that he would be allowed on deck, or that his comrade would be restored to him; but, as the weary hours dragged slowly by without either of these things happening, these hopes grew fainter and fainter until finally they vanished.

When food and water were brought to him, he drank of the latter but refused to eat, although the food was fresh meat, the first he had seen since the dreadful day when he had been enticed aboard the ship. It was another proof that they were once more near land. Perhaps even now the forest for which he longed was close at hand, and perhaps people of his own race were come off to trade. Perhaps Tasquanto, who had picked up a number of English words, was acting as interpreter for them. In that case he would doubtless find a chance for escape, though even if he should, Nahma was certain that he would not make use of it. Were they not brothers, sworn to share each other's fortunes, good or ill, to the end? No! Tasquanto would never desert him; but sooner or later, if he were still alive, would come again to him. Of this our lad was certain.

After a while the lonely prisoner fell asleep, and when he next awoke the ship was again in motion. He felt about for his companion, but could not find him; he called aloud, but got no answer. Then he knew that he was indeed alone in the world and that something terrible must have happened to Tasquanto. When next he was allowed on deck he looked eagerly for his friend, and, seeing nothing of him, relapsed into a condition of apathy. He no longer cared what happened, and refused to eat the food offered him.

"Won't eat, eh?" growled Captain Dermer, on learning of this state of affairs. "We'll see about that."

The grizzled old mariner's method of seeing about things was so effective that the refractory young Indian shortly found himself pinned to the deck by two sailors. A third pinched his nose, and when he opened his mouth for breath poured in hot soup that the victim was obliged to swallow to keep from choking. So he was fed by force, and his strength was sustained until the ship once more came to anchor.

As usual, Nahma was confined below when this happened, and when he was next brought on deck he was given no time to look about him before being seized, stripped of the foul garments that he had worn during the voyage, and scrubbed from head to foot, roughly but thoroughly. Then he was provided with a new suit of buckskin that had been acquired by trade from the Abenakis. He was also given colors and a mirror and ordered to paint his face. Showing symptoms of disobedience, he was made to understand that one of the crew would do it for him; and, rather than be thus disfigured, he reluctantly complied. After he had satisfactorily decorated himself, greatly to the amusement of the crew, he was left to his own devices and allowed to wander about the deck as he pleased.

Gaining a position where he could see beyond the ship's side, he was as amazed and bewildered as though he had been transported to another planet, for the vessel had ascended the Thames, and his outlook was upon London.

Not a tree was to be seen, not a green thing, only houses, until it seemed as though the whole world must be covered with them. Even the river disappeared beneath houses built in a double row on a bridge that spanned it a short distance away. The ship was moored beside a great dingy building, from and into which men came and went as thickly as bees swarming about a hollow tree in his native woods.

Although no such clouds of smoke hung above London then as infold it to-day, there was enough to impress our young savage with the belief that a forest fire must be raging just beyond the buildings that obstructed his view. This belief was strengthened by the ceaseless roar of the city, that, to him, held the same elements of terror as the awful voice of a wide-spread conflagration.

If Tasquanto were only with him that they might discuss these things. But, alas! he was alone, as unfitted for a life-struggle amid those heretofore undreamed-of surroundings as a newborn babe, and, like it, unprovided with a language understandable by those about him. Set down in the heart of a primeval forest he would have been perfectly at home; but face to face with this hideous wilderness of human construction he was appalled at his own insignificance and utter helplessness.

As he turned away terror-stricken he noticed that several persons gathered about Captain Dermer were regarding him curiously. One of them, a young man of about Nahma's own age, apparently touched by the hopeless expression on our lad's painted face, stepped towards him with outstretched hand.

"Winslow," he said, pointing to himself.

"Massasoit," answered the other, promptly, and indicating his own person.

Although he could not understand the newcomer's words he appreciated the hearty grip of his hand, and, gazing into his honest eyes, felt that here was one who might become a friend.

"What are you going to do with him?" inquired Winslow, stepping back beside Captain Dermer.

"Let him go when he can pay his passage-money, or turn him over to the first person who will pay it for him," was the reply.

"What is the sum?"

"Twenty pounds, no more nor less."

"I have not that amount with me, but if you will give me a day or two I think I can get it. Will you keep him until I come again?"

"Unless some other turns up in the mean time equally desirous of accommodating him."

"Captain, I vill pay the money on the spot," exclaimed a voice, and wheeling about, Winslow saw a man of sporty aspect arrayed in tawdry imitation of a gentleman, and of a decidedly Hebraic cast of countenance. He was extending a handful of gold pieces, which Captain Dermer took and counted.

"It is a trade," he said. "Take him and may luck go with you."

Thus was sold, in the city of London, a free-born native American; and he was but one of many New World people who shared a similar fate both before and afterwards.

CHAPTER XX

ONE FRIENDLY FACE

The man who on pretence of paying Nahma's passage-money had in reality bought him was a well-known London fur-dealer, who had visited the ship to appraise her cargo. The young fellow who had extended to our forlorn lad the hand of friendship, and who, but for lack of ready means, would have redeemed him from a threatened slavery, was a Mr. Edward Winslow. He was the youngest son of a well-to-do Devon family, who had taken a degree at Oxford and was now reading law in the Temple. He was intensely interested in America and everything pertaining to it. Thus, on hearing that a ship just arrived from the New World was in the Thames, he hastened to board her, that he might converse with those who had so recently trod the shores he longed to visit. Nahma was the first American he had ever seen, and he regarded him with a lively curiosity that was changed to pity at sight of his hopeless face. Now he turned fiercely on the Jew who by payment of a paltry sum of money had become master of the young stranger's fate.

"What do you intend to do with him?" he asked.

"Vat vould you have done mit him yourself had your purse been as full as your stomach?" asked the other, impudently.

"I would have found for him a home in which he might be taught Christianity and civilization, and then I would have taken the first opportunity for sending him back to his own land."

"Mayhap those be the very things I also vould do by the young heathen; who knows?" replied the furrier, with a leer. "At any rate, I have charge of him now, and vill take him at once to my happy home. You may set him ashore for me, captain."

"Not I," responded Captain Dermer. "I have no longer aught to do with him. Take him ashore yourself."

Thus confronted with his new responsibility, the man approached Nahma and, seizing him roughly by an arm, said, "Come mit me, heathen."

With a quick motion the young Indian wrenched himself free and faced his new master with so fierce a look that the latter involuntarily quailed beneath it and stepped back.

"Ah!" he snarled, "that's your game, is it? Ve'll see who comes out best."

With this he called to some men of his employ who were hoisting out bales of furs and bade them come to him, bringing a stout cord.

"Hold!" cried Winslow, stepping beside the young Indian. "See you not that he is desperate, and that if you try to bind him there will be bloodshed? He will surely kill you, if he dies for it the next moment. Leave him to me and I will guarantee to take him where you may desire, only I give you warning to treat him decently and without violence."

Thus saying the speaker held out his hand to Nahma, and by signs intimated that he was to accompany him.

By instinct the young American had recognized this youth as a friend, and now he unhesitatingly left the ship in his company.

As a mob would have been attracted by the appearance of an American Indian in the crowded streets, a covered cart belonging to the furrier was procured, and in it our lad was driven to a rear entrance of his master's shop, which fronted on a fashionable thoroughfare, while the others reached the same place on foot.

During that bewildering ride Nahma sat with stolid face but with keen eyes, taking in all the marvellous details of his surroundings. Next to the throngs of people hurrying to and fro along the narrow, crooked, and ill-paved streets, the appearance of horses most impressed him, for never had he seen beasts at once so large and so completely under the control of man.

No word passed between Winslow and the furrier until their destination was reached. Then the latter asked, sneeringly,—

"Now, me lud, vat vill your 'ighness do next?"

"I will go inside and see him disposed," replied the young man, calmly.

"Oh, vell, come in and view the royal apartments," said the other, willing to have Winslow continue his responsibility until the new acquisition was safely housed.

So the young Indian was taken from the cart and led into the shop, causing a buzz of excitement among the few who saw him climbing a narrow back stairway. He was finally guided to a small chamber directly beneath the roof and lighted by a single window that could not be opened. Had it not been for Winslow's reassuring presence, Nahma would have refused to ascend those stairs, which, being the first he had ever encountered, filled him with dismay.

After Winslow had seen the stranger in whom he took so great an interest thus safely placed for the present and the furrier had locked the door on his captive, the two descended again to the shop.

"What will you now do with him?" asked the former.

"It may be I vill train him to my business and send him out to America as a fur-buyer," answered the other. "Maybe I vill keep him as a curiosity. I have not yet decided; but vatever I do is no concern of yours."

"Will you sell him to me?"

"Maybe so ven I see your money."

With this Winslow was forced to be content, and he departed with the hope of redeeming his newly made friend and of carrying out his vaguely formed intentions concerning him. Although twenty pounds was not a large sum, it would embarrass him to procure it, since his family, though well-to-do, were not people of wealth, and he was living on a monthly allowance so small as barely to support him in gentility.

In the mean time Nahma, left to his own melancholy company, gazed from his window over the roofs and chimney-pots of London, feeling that no greater evils could possibly befall him, and yet wondering vaguely what would happen next. Food was brought to him and water, but no change in his situation took place until the following morning.

Then his master appeared accompanied by a coarse-featured man of evident strength, whom the furrier had engaged to be keeper of his new treasure. By them the young Indian was taken down to the shop, where a small platform had been prepared for him. It was covered and surrounded with costly furs, and here Nahma was seated with a fur robe draped across his shoulders. Close at hand stood his keeper to see that he neither escaped nor did injury to any about him. With the tableau arranged, a stout 'prentice lad took a stand just outside the street entrance and cried in lusty tones the novel attraction to be seen within.

"Step this way, lords and ladies. Come all ye gentlefolk, attend the reception of his Highness, a native American cannibal prince just arrived from the New World. Look within! Look within! Under the sign of the Ermine Royal sits he. Free of charge are all gentlefolk invited to meet him. This way, lords and ladies. Look within!"

To this novel reception none but the well-dressed and evidently well-to-do were admitted, since the poor could not be expected to purchase furs then any more than now. And there would have been no room for them in the limited space of the dingy little shop even had they been admitted, for ere long it was crowded with fashionable folk eager to be entertained by a novelty, while their retainers filled the street. The spectators stared at Nahma and listened with credulous ears to the marvellous tales told concerning him by the furrier, who, clad in gorgeous raiment, acted the parts of host and showman. Also many of them purchased furs, which was more to the purpose. Never had the Ermine Royal done such a business, and never had its proprietor greater reason to be satisfied with a venture.

Amid all came Edward Winslow with his twenty pounds, which he proffered to the Jew in return for Nahma's release. But the latter laughed him to scorn.

"For twenty pund did you think to get him, me lud? Nay, that was the price I paid, as you vell know, and I must at least double my money. Forty pund is my lowest offer, and fifty if he continues to attract trade as at present. Speech mit him? I have no objection, only have a care that you seek not to seduce him from my service, or a thing might happen not to your liking."

Keenly disappointed at this result of his undertaking, the young man pushed his way through the crowd until he stood close to the platform, when he called, softly,—

"Massasoit."

Instantly a glad light flashed into the eyes of the dejected figure thus set up for a show, and, turning eagerly in that direction, he exclaimed,—

"Winslow."

Then the two friends clasped hands, and Winslow managed to convey the information that he would come again on the morrow.

He kept his promise; and, though he had not succeeded in securing the money necessary to redeem the young Indian, his visit brought much comfort. For many days thereafter he came regularly, often bringing some little thing that he thought might give pleasure; and these daily glimpses of a friendly face were the only rays of light penetrating the unhappy darkness of Nahma's captivity. He was never allowed to leave the building, and was only marched to and fro up and down those weary stairs between the den in which he lived and the hated platform on which he was exhibited to gaping customers.

At the end of three weeks Winslow, having received his month's allowance and so raised the necessary forty pounds, tendered it to the fur-dealer for the release of his slave, only to be told that the price had again been doubled.

Upon this the young man flew into a rage and there was an exchange of bitter words, that ended in Winslow being told to mind his own affairs and not attempt an interference with those that did not concern him. As several 'prentice lads had gathered near during this quarrel and stood eagerly awaiting their master's permission to pounce upon the stranger, he realized the weakness of his position, and prudently ended the affair by withdrawing from the scene. At the same time he was as determined as ever to effect Nahma's deliverance, and that speedily.

For this purpose he invited a number of the more reckless of his Temple companions to a dinner, at which he told the story of Massasoit and enlisted their sympathies in his behalf. Then he proposed a rescue, to which they enthusiastically agreed.

According to this plan they were to meet near the furrier's shop at the busiest hour of the second day from then, each man wearing his sword, and prepared to use it if necessary. There they were to mingle with the sightseers and resist any attempts at interference with the movements of Winslow. The latter undertook to spirit the young Indian out of the same rear entrance through which he had first been brought, into an unfrequented alley, while one of his friends should for a moment distract the attention of the keeper.

To perfect the details of this scheme and provide a safe retreat for him whom they proposed to rescue occupied two days, and then all was in readiness. At this point the would-be rescuers were confronted by an unforeseen and insurmountable obstacle. The young Indian had disappeared. He was no longer an inmate of the furrier's shop, and no one could or would give the slightest information concerning him.

CHAPTER XXI

A CHANGE OF MASTERS

For some days Nahma's master had been uneasy about him. Close confinement, lack of exercise and fresh air, and a hopeless melancholy were so telling upon the captive that his health was seriously affected. He was thin and miserable, had no appetite, and suffered from a hacking cough. These things troubled the fur-dealer, not because of his humanity, for he had none, but because of a prospect of losing the money he had invested in this bit of perishable property. He was also alarmed by Winslow's interest in the young Indian, and feared the very thing that the former had planned.

Then, too, one of his gentleman customers had suggested that when the fact of an American prince being in London came to the king's ears he would probably order him to be brought to the palace. In that case, as the furrier well knew, he would never be recompensed for his outlay, since King James was not given to spending unnecessary money, and he might even be called to account for holding a royal personage in captivity. He wished now that he had not described his Indian as a prince; and, all things considered, decided that the sooner he got rid of him the better off he would be.

It happened that while he was in this frame of mind he was visited by a travelling mountebank, whose business was to exhibit freaks and curiosities of whatsoever kind he could obtain, at country fairs. Having heard of the fur-dealer's Indian, he went to see him, and was so impressed with his value as an attraction that he promptly offered ten pounds for him.

"Already haf I refused forty," replied the furrier.

"It was doubtless offered when he was in condition. Now, as any one may see, he is on the verge of a quick decline and is like to die on your hands. It would be a risk to take him at any price, and it will cost a pretty penny to restore him to health, without which he is of no more value than a mangy dog."

"But I haf advanced twenty pund for his passage-money, and haf been at the expense of his keep ever since."

"A cost that has been repaid a thousand-fold by the advertisement he has given your wares. But to insure you against loss, which I well know a Jew hates worse than death itself, I will give twenty pounds for the varlet, sick and scrawny though he be. What say you? Is it a bargain?"

"Hand over the price and he is yours."

Of course the subject of this barter was not consulted concerning it. Nor did he know anything of the change about to come over his life until darkness had fallen. Then, as he lay on his bed of musty straw, dreaming of the free forest life that was once his, he was startled by the entrance into his room of two men, one of whom bore a rush-light. In him Nahma recognized his hated keeper, but the other was a stranger.

"Come," said the former, gruffly; and, glad of any break in the deadly monotony of his life, Nahma obediently followed him, while the other brought up the rear.

Down-stairs they went and out into the darkness of the streets, where each of the men grasped him by an arm as though fearful that he might attempt an escape. The young Indian smiled bitterly as he realized this, for nothing was further from his thought. In all that wilderness of houses he had but one friend, and he knew no more where to look for Winslow than he would if the latter were dead. To him all other white men represented cruelty and injustice, therefore nothing was to be gained by escaping from those who held him. He would only fall into the clutches of others against whom he would be equally powerless. So he went along quietly and with apparent willingness, somewhat to the surprise of his new master.

"I fail to note but that he goes readily enough," he remarked. "Methought you said he was vicious and like to prove troublesome."

"Oh, he's quiet enough now," replied the other, "but wait and see. They're as treacherous, these Hammerican savages, as cats. Purr till they see a good chance and then scratch. If they draw life's blood they're all the more pleased. I knows 'em, for I've had experience, and my word! but you've got to watch 'em every minute."

It was by such representations that the keeper hoped to induce the showman to continue him in his present easy position. Now he wished that his charge would make some aggressive exhibition merely to demonstrate the necessity for his own presence. He slyly pinched the prisoner's arm until it was ready to bleed, with the hope of at least causing him to cry out; but Nahma endured the pain with all the stoicism of his race and gave no sign.

Thus they proceeded through a weary labyrinth of foul streets, only lighted at long intervals by flaring torches borne by retainers of well-to-do pedestrians, until finally they turned into the yard of a rambling tavern that stood on the outskirts of the town. It was a famous resort for wagoners who transported goods to and from all parts of the kingdom, and its court was now crowded with ponderous vehicles and their lading.

Here Nahma was thrust for safe-keeping into an outhouse, the air of which was close and foul, and its door was barred behind him. To our unhappy lad it seemed as if the whole remainder of his life was to be marked only by a succession of imprisonments, each more dismal than its predecessor. In Quebec he had had Tasquanto's companionship and an open window. On shipboard he had been given the same comrade and a daily outing. In the furrier's establishment he had had a window and an occasional hand-clasp from Winslow; but here he was alone, in absolute darkness, and gasping for a breath of fresh air.

The wretched night finally came to an end, and with the first gray of morning his new master appeared, bringing an armful of coarse clothing, soiled and worn. Stripping Nahma of his buckskin suit, he compelled him to don these ill-fitting garments, and then left him a platter of bones for his breakfast.

A little later they were on the road, and, to his amazement, Nahma found himself leading a bear. It was a big brown bear, and its whole head was enclosed in a stout muzzle; but, in spite of this, our young Indian, who had never heard of a tame bear, felt anything but comfortable at finding himself in such company unarmed. Besides himself and the bear, the party was made up of the showman, a cadaverous youth answering to the name of "Blink," who afterwards proved to be a contortionist, and a heavily laden pack-horse. To Nahma's relief, the big man who had acted as his keeper was no longer of the company.

For a time our lad was so taken up with his bear and the discomforts of his unaccustomed clothing that he paid but slight attention to his surroundings. Then, all of a sudden, he uttered a cry of amazed delight, for they were entering a forest. No longer were houses to be seen, no longer was the horrid din of the city to be heard. Once more was he beneath green trees, with the songs of birds ringing in his ears and the smell of the woods in his nostrils. He drew in long breaths of the scented air, and a new light came into his eyes. Having found a forest, might he not also hope to discover people of his own kind? If there were forests in this strange land and bears, why should there not also be Indians? At any rate, he would keep a sharp watch, and if he should see any, how quickly he would take leave of his present companions and join them!

That night they lay at an inn, where an iron shackle was locked about one of Nahma's ankles, and, with the bear, he was chained up in a stable. On the following day they reached a straggling country town in which a fair was to be held and where they were to give an exhibition. Here they pitched a tent. Nahma's suit of buckskin was restored to him, and he was again made to paint his face.

In this first exhibition he had nothing to do but stand and be stared at by curious rustics, but after this he was taught and encouraged to perform a number of acts in company with the bear. One of these was to shoot, with bow and arrow, an apple, or some other small object, from the animal's head.

Then they would wrestle together, and finally a sort of a dance was arranged for them, in which Blink, made up as a clown for the occasion, also took part. Thus the show became so unique and popular that its proprietor coined more money than any other on the road.

But with prosperity came an evil more terrible even than adversity; for, with money to spend, the showman began to squander it in gambling and drinking until it was a rare thing for him to draw a sober breath. He became quarrelsome with his intimates and brutal to those in his power. His poor bear was beaten and tortured to make it learn new tricks until it became a snarling, morose beast, influenced only by fear, and dangerous to all except the young Indian, who was its fellow-sufferer. He, too, was abused, starved, beaten, and in all ways maltreated for not learning faster and pouring more money into his master's bottomless pockets.

One day, while Nahma and the bear were wearily performing their antics before a crowd of gaping yokels in the market-place of a small shire town in the west, the youth's attention was drawn to a child who was uttering shrill cries of pleasure. She was a dainty little thing with flaxen hair and blue eyes, exquisitely dressed, and was in charge of a maid. They had come from a coach that was drawn up before a shop near by, and the throng had opened to make way for them until they stood in the very front rank.

Suddenly the child, in an ecstasy of delight, pulled away from her nurse and ran forward with the evident intention of caressing the bear as though he had been a big dog. The brute was so tired, hungry, and cross that Nahma had with difficulty kept him to his work. Now, with a snarl and a fierce gleam in his small bloodshot eyes, he raised a threatening paw as though to sweep away the little fluttering thing that came running so confidently towards him.

A great cry rose from the crowd. The maid, so terrified as to be incapable of motion, screamed and covered her face with her hands; but Nahma, darting forward, snatched the child from under the descending paw. So narrow was the escape that his left arm was torn from shoulder to elbow by the cruel claws, and he staggered beneath the blow.

The showman, who had been passing his cap among the spectators, ran to the bear and, beating him over the head with a stout cudgel, drove him to his quarters in a near-by stable. Part of the populace cheered Nahma, while others demanded the death of the bear, and amid all the confusion came the mother of the little girl, frantic with terror. To her our lad delivered the child, frightened but unharmed. Then, without waiting to be rewarded, or even thanked, he ran to look after his friend the bear.

CHAPTER XXII

NAHMA AND THE BEAR RUN AWAY

Nahma found the showman and Blink engaged in a violent dispute over the bear. The former was insisting that Blink should escape, with the animal, from the rear of the stable and lead it to a place of concealment on the outskirts of the village, where he would join them later. In the mean time he would divert the attention of the mob until the escape could be made. Blink, who was not on friendly terms with the bear, was refusing on the ground that, with the animal in its present temper, his life would not be worth a moment's purchase.

"Then let the heathen take him, and do you go along to see that they do not give us the slip," exclaimed the man, as Nahma appeared and a howl from the mob announced their approach. Their interest had been distracted for a minute while they watched the lady with the frightened child in her arms regain her coach, which was immediately driven away. Now they were ready to settle with the bear, and turned towards the stable in which he had taken refuge. As they drew near the showman, who, though a brute, was no coward, appeared in its open doorway and confronted them.

"Good my masters," he cried, "what seek you?"

"Thy bear!" roared a dozen voices. "Bring forth thy bear that we may bait him. He is not fit to live, and must be slain."

Again the showman attempted to speak, but his voice was drowned in the bedlam of cries raised by the mob; and, losing control of his temper, he shook his cudgel defiantly at them. Upon this a shower of stones was hurled at him, and one of them striking him on the head, he staggered and fell. At this the mob halted, and some even sneaked away, fearful of consequences. The village barber, who was also its surgeon, bustled forward to make an examination of the wounded man. He was conscious, but in spite of, or possibly on account of, copious bloodletting, which was the only remedy administered, he died a few hours later.

So completely was public attention distracted by this tragic event, that for a time no thought was given to the original cause of the disturbance, and, finally, when search was made for the bear, he was nowhere to be seen. Not until the following day was any trace discovered of those who had been in the showman's company. Then the one known as "Blink" was found on the edge of a wood, helplessly bound and half dead from a night of cold and terror. He could only tell that, having escaped with the bear and the heathen, the latter had suddenly set upon him without warning or provocation and reduced him to the condition in which he was discovered. What had become of them or whither they had gone he knew not, nor did he care. He only hoped he would never again set eyes on the savage monsters who were so unfit for Christian company.

In the mean time Nahma and his companions had found no difficulty in leaving the village unnoticed, since all public attention was for the moment drawn in the opposite direction. Thus they successfully gained the woodland that had been appointed by the showman as a place of rendezvous. Here the young American suddenly realized that only Blink stood between him and the freedom for which he longed. Up to this time he had been shackled at night and so closely watched by day that no chance of escape had offered. Now one had come, and so quick was our lad to take advantage of it that within a minute the unsuspecting Blink was lying helplessly bound hand and foot with his own kerchief and a sash that formed part of his professional costume. Thus was he left, while Nahma and the bear, whom the former now regarded as his sole friend in all the world, plunged into the forest depths and disappeared.

The England of that long-ago date was a very different country from the England of to-day, and its entire population hardly exceeded two millions of souls. Its few cities were small, and connected by highways so abominable that travellers frequently lost their way while trying to follow them. Not more than one-quarter of the arable lands were under cultivation, while the remainder was covered with dark forests and great fens, marshes, and desolate moors across which one might journey for a day without sight of human habitation. Game of all kinds abounded, and its hunting formed the chief recreation of the gentry and of those nobles who left London during a portion of the year to dwell on their estates.

Thus our young Indian, upon gaining his freedom, found himself amid surroundings at once familiar and congenial. He had with him the bow and arrows used in his recent exhibitions, a fire-bag containing flint, steel, and tinder, and a dirk that had been taken from Blink. Thus provided he had no anxiety on the score of maintaining himself comfortably. He realized that the bear was an encumbrance, but in his present loneliness he was loath to part from it. And so the two pushed on together until they had penetrated several miles into the forest, when darkness overtook them.

Then Nahma made a fire beside a small stream and cooked a rabbit he had shot an hour earlier, while the bear nosed about for acorns, grubs, and edible roots.

They continued to traverse the forest on the following day, keeping to the same general direction until our lad was satisfied that he was beyond danger from pursuit, when he began to look about for a supper and a camping-place. Both of these came at the same time, for on discovering, successfully stalking, and finally killing a deer, he found that the animal had been drinking from a spring of clear water, beside which he determined to establish his camp. Further than this he had no plans. It was enough for the present that he was free, in the forest that he loved, and beyond all knowledge of the white man whom he hated. Here, then, he would abide for a time, or until he should discover people of his own kind, for he was still impressed with the belief that others like himself must inhabit those game-filled forests.

That night both he and the bear, to whom he talked as though it were a human being, ate to their satisfaction of deer meat, and Nahma lay down to sleep beside his shaggy friend, happier than he had been at any time since leaving his native land.

The next morning he was early astir and ready to begin work on the lodge that he proposed to construct. By mid-day he had the poles of the frame cut, set in the ground, arched over until they met, and fastened in position. Then he went in quest of proper material for a thatch or covering. The bear, having spent the morning in feeding, was left behind, chained to a small tree and fast asleep.

While searching for the material he wanted Nahma struck the fresh trail of a deer, which after a long chase he overtook and killed. As he was returning with the hide and haunches on his back he was startled by a baying of hounds, which changed as he listened to a snarling, growling, and yelping that indicated a battle royal. From the nature and direction of these sounds our lad realized that trouble of some kind had come to the bear, and, without a thought of danger to himself, he ran to the assistance of his comrade. Reaching the scene, he found the bear, though sadly hampered by his chain, making a gallant fight against a pack of boar-hounds that had come across him while ranging the forest. They were fierce, gaunt creatures, and although two of their number, already knocked out, were lying to one side feebly licking their wounds, it was evident that the chained bear was overmatched and must speedily be dragged down. Flinging away his burden and drawing his dirk, Nahma rushed forward and sprang into the thick of the fray, uttering the fierce war-cry of the Iroquois as he did so.

For a few minutes there was a furious and indiscriminate mingling of bear, dogs, and man, then of a sudden the young Indian was seized from behind, dragged backward, and flung to the ground by one of two men clad in the green dress of foresters, who had just arrived on the scene. While Nahma's assailant hastily but securely fastened the lad's arms so as to render him harmless, the other ranger ended the battle, still raging, by thrusting a keen-bladed boar-spear through the bear's body. It pierced the animal's heart, and he sank with a sobbing groan.

"A fair sorrowful bit o' wark this, Jean," remarked the man who had killed the bear, as he examined the several dogs. "Fower dead; two killed by yon brute and two by the dirk of this wastrel. All the rest gouged, cut, and bit up. But he'll answer for it smartly when once Sir Amory claps eyes on him, the thievin', murthren gypsy poacher."

"Yes, I reckon he'll sweat fine," replied the other, with a grin; "but did iver thou see bear chained afore?"

"Noa, niver. Lucky thing 'twas, though. But come on whoam. Bring Poacher with 'e, and we'll send pack-horse for bear. No use looking furder for pigs this day."

So poor Nahma, once more bereft of his freedom and of the dumb brute whom he regarded as his only friend, his garments rent and his body bleeding from a dozen wounds, was marched away between the two stout rangers, while after them trooped the dogs.

Sir Amory Effingham, a knight in high favor at court, was lord of that region, and being devoted to the chase, he spent several months of each year at Garnet Hall, the ivy-covered forest castle in which his family had been cradled for generations. It lay a league from the scene of Nahma's capture, and by the time he was brought within sight of its battlemented towers the short day was closing and night was at hand.

While one of the rangers kennelled the dogs and looked after their wounds, the other thrust Nahma, with his hurts still unattended, into an empty store-room, locked its door, and went to make report of what had taken place.

"A gypsy, eh? A poacher, caught red-handed, and a dog-killer, is he?" quoth Sir Amory, angrily. "Hanging will be too good for him. He should be drawn and quartered as an example to all of his kidney, and I will deal with his case in the morning. Look well to him, then, see that he escapes not, and bring him to me in the great hall after the breaking of fast."

"Yes, Sir Amory."

"And, Jean, send for that bear and have his pelt taken before the body stiffens."

"Yes, Sir Amory."

"Also, Jean, give both the dogs and the prisoner a good feed of bear's meat."

So all was done as directed; only Nahma, realizing the nature of the food thrown to him some hours later, refused to eat of it.

CHAPTER XXIII

AN HONORED GUEST

On the following morning, after the lord of the manor, his family, and all his retainers had partaken of their rude but abundant breakfast, and washed it down with copious draughts of ale, which at that time took the place of coffee or tea, Sir Amory ordered the prisoner of the preceding evening to be brought before him. The dining-tables, which were merely boards laid on trestles, were cleared away, and the great hall was made ready to serve as a court of justice. Witnesses were summoned, and spectators gathered, until but few of the knight's following were absent. Squires, pages, men-at-arms, grooms, foresters, and under-servants, all filled with an eager curiosity, flocked to the scene of trial; for the case in hand was of so serious a nature that its resulting punishment would be certain to afford vast entertainment.

In those days the killing of a deer by any person beneath the rank of a gentleman was a capital offence; while the killing of a hunting dog by one of the peasant class ranked as a crime so abominable as to merit the severest penalty. For either of these things the offender might be hanged, whipped to death, or executed in any other fitting manner, at the discretion of the judge. He might not be beheaded, as that form of punishment was reserved for offences against the state, committed by persons of rank. Neither might he be burned, since the stake was only for witches and victims of religious persecution. If the lord of the manor were inclined to be merciful, the deer-stealer or dog-killer might be given his life, and escape with some such slight punishment as having his ears cropped or a hand chopped off; but in the present case it was universally agreed that the crime was of a nature to demand the severest possible punishment. Thus, when the prisoner appeared, he was regarded with eager curiosity as one who promised to furnish a spectacle of uncommon interest.

Friendless, wounded, ragged, half starved, and utterly ignorant of the situation confronting him, the son of Longfeather was led the whole length of the great hall to the dais at its upper end, on which sat the master of his fate. As he was halted, Sir Amory exclaimed,—

"On my soul, as scurvy a knave as ever I set eyes upon. I knew not that even a gypsy could present so foul an aspect. What is thy name and condition, sirrah?"

Not understanding what was said, Nahma made no answer. Only, recalling the teaching of his own people, he stared his questioner full in the face with a mien that, in spite of his sorry plight, was quite as haughty as that of the knight himself.

"A contumacious varlet and insolent," remarked Sir Amory, "but it is possible that we may find means to lower his pride. Let the ranger named Jem stand forth and relate his tale of the occurrence concerning which this investigation is made."

So Jem told his story, and it was corroborated by the other forester. Also were the dead hounds introduced as evidence, together with the dirk that Nahma had used so effectively.

"What hast thou to say in thy own behalf, scoundrel?" asked the knight, turning again to the prisoner after all this testimony against him had been submitted.

Still there was no answer, but only an unflinching gaze and a proudly uplifted head.

"Think you the creature is dumb?" inquired the puzzled magistrate.

"No, Sir Amory," replied one of the foresters, "of a surety he is not, for we heard him call loudly to the bear, and at sound of his voice the beast made violent effort to break his chain that he might get to him."

"Chain?" quoth the knight. "This is the first mention I have heard of any chain. What mean you? Was the bear indeed chained?"

"Chained and muzzled was he," admitted the ranger, "else it had gone more hardly with the dogs than happened."

"Chained and muzzled," repeated the knight, reflectively, and casting a searching gaze upon the prisoner. "Still, it may be only a coincidence." With this he gave an order in a low tone to a page who stood at hand, and the boy darted away.

"Saw you trace of other gypsies at or near that place?" asked the knight, continuing his examination of the forester.

"No, Sir Amory. That is, we saw no humans, but there was a booth partly built close at hand."

"What is the material of the prisoner's dress?"

"Deer-skin, Sir Amory, nothing less."

At this moment a tapestry was drawn aside, and a lady, appearing on the dais, stood beside her husband with a look of inquiry. She was followed by one bearing in her arms a child, at sight of which the prisoner was surprised into a momentary start as of recognition.

"My dear," said Sir Amory, "will you favor us by glancing at yonder gypsy and telling if ever you have set eyes on him before?"

The lady looked in the direction indicated, but shook her head. Ere she could speak, however, the maid, who had followed her gaze, uttered a cry, and exclaimed,—

"It is the very one, my lady. The youth, I mean, who danced with that dreadful bear and saved the life of my little mistress."

"Yes," said the lady, slowly. "I did not recognize him on the moment; but now me-thinks he is the same from whose hands I received my child, safe and unharmed, though blood-bespattered. But, Amory, what is he doing here? A prisoner and under guard! Surely——"

"It is all a mistake," cried the knight, rising to his feet in great agitation. "He is not a prisoner, but an honored guest. Nor is he under guard, but under the protection of one who owes to him a life dearer than his own. Gentlemen, the hearing is dismissed; the prisoner is honorably acquitted, and will hereafter be known as my friend, if indeed he can forgive the cruel wrong I meditated against him. Away, ye varlets. Bring food and wine. Fetch warm water and clean napery, salve and liniments. Body o' me! The youth is wounded and hath had no attention. He looks ready to drop with weakness. Draw a settle for him beside the fire. Fetch——"

But the servants were already flying in every direction in their efforts to minister to the evident needs of him whose position had undergone so sudden a transformation.

At the same time Nahma himself was even more bewildered by the good fortune that was overwhelming him than ever by the hard fate that had for so long been his constant attendant.

Somewhat later the lady who, with her companions, had withdrawn, came again to the hall, and stepping to where she could obtain a good view of the youth, looked at him steadily for the space of a minute. He, in the mean time, had been bathed and fed, his wounds had been dressed, and he wore a body-gown from the knight's own wardrobe that gave him an air of grace and dignity.

"He is no gypsy, Sir Amory," said the lady, finally, withdrawing her gaze and turning to her husband.

"I myself am beginning to doubt if he belongs to those nomads," replied the knight. "But if not a gypsy, to what race can he lay claim, with that tinge of color and with hair of such raven blackness?"

"Dost remember the tale told us in London by my cousin Edward concerning an arrival from the New World in whom he had taken an interest?"

"Ay, well do I, and it so aroused my curiosity that I made an errand shortly after to the place where he was said to be, but he had disappeared. How was he called? Can you remember the name?"

"He was called 'Massasoit,'" replied the lady, uttering the word distinctly and observing the youth as she spoke.

Turning quickly he looked at her with eager questioning.

"Who are your friends?" she asked, addressing him directly and speaking the words slowly.

He understood and answered, "Bear frien'. Tasquanto frien'. White man frien', Winslow."

"That proves it!" cried the lady, triumphantly. "He must be the American Indian of whom Cousin Edward told us, and who is said to be a prince in his own country. At any rate, as he certainly saved the life of our child, we have ample reason to befriend him."

"Indeed, yes," agreed Sir Amory. "And to fail in a duty so plainly indicated would lay us open to the charge of base ingratitude."

Thus it happened that the young American who had been kidnapped from his own country, sold as a slave in London, and finally arrested on a charge that threatened to cost him his life, became the honored guest of a stately English home. His hosts sought in every way to promote his comfort and happiness, and when they discovered that he preferred living in the open to dwelling under a roof, he was promptly given the freedom of their domain. He was also accorded full liberty to dwell on it where he pleased, and to kill such of its abundant game as would supply his needs. Armed with this permission, Nahma immediately repaired to the place where he had already begun the building of a lodge after the fashion of his own people, and completed it to his satisfaction as well as that of his hosts, who took a lively interest in his work. He covered it with bark and lined its interior with the skins of fur-bearing animals. In the centre was his fireplace, and at one side his couch of dry sedge-grass covered with the great shaggy hide of his one-time friend, the bear. Here our Indian dwelt almost as contentedly as though in his own land and under the trees of his native forest.

Much of his time was devoted to accompanying Sir Amory on his hunting expeditions, during which the youth's marvellous skill in tracking game and his fearlessness in moments of peril won for him both admiration and respect.

On days when there was no hunting he busied himself with making bows, arrows, or snow-shoes, and in receiving visits from the green-coated foresters, whose tastes and pursuits were so similar to his own. He taught them some things, but learned more than he taught; and chiefest of all the things that he learned was to load and fire a musket. Thus was solved the mystery of the white man's thunder-stick, and he could now smile as he recalled the melancholy experience of Tasquanto and himself in attempting to fire a salute.

So some months were happily passed, and it seemed as though our young American would spend the remainder of his life as an English forester. Then all of a sudden there occurred an amazing thing, by which he was rendered so unhappy that he no longer cared to live if the balance of his days must be passed under existing conditions.

CHAPTER XXIV

NAHMA REMEMBERS

Most welcome of all the guests at Nahma's lodge was the little lady Betty, who was sometimes taken thither by her father mounted in front of him on his great Flemish horse Baldric. A strong friendship had sprung up between the child and the young Indian, and she was never happier than during the hour occasionally spent with him. She always brought some little gift, and he never failed to have ready a unique bit of his own handiwork to offer in return. Once it was a wee bow and a quiver of small stone-headed arrows. Again he presented her with the beautifully dressed skin of an otter. At length he completed a pair of tiny snow-shoes gayly fringed and ornamented. For some days after they were finished he waited expectantly the coming of his little friend, and as she failed to appear, he finally decided to take his gift to the castle.

Now, it happened that Sir Amory, being called by some business to the near-by city of Bristol, had taken his wife and little daughter with him for a brief visit, from which they had just returned. As was usual on such occasions, they had brought back a number of trifling gifts for members of the household, and also one for the young Indian whom they held in such high esteem.

The city of Bristol, more than any other in England, was building up a trade with the New World. While this trade was more especially with the Virginia plantations, it was gradually extending northward along the American coast. Thus a ship, recently returned, had voyaged as far north as the French settlements, trading with natives wherever found on her way. This ship had brought back many curious things, among which was an object of native make that Sir Amory, having his Indian guest in his mind, purchased on sight.

"It may interest him," he said to his wife, "and, at any rate, it will be something for Betty to take him when next she and I ride to his lodge." So this present was fetched home with the others, and was to have been carried out to Nahma on the very day of his appearance at the castle.

On learning that the Indian waited outside with a gift for Betty, Sir Amory ordered him to be brought in. The knight and his lady together with several guests were grouped near the huge fireplace in the great hall as Nahma entered and, advancing gravely, extended a hand to his host. Then, looking about inquiringly, he pronounced the single word "Betty."

"I' faith!" laughed the knight, "the young man hath quickly recognized the most important personage of this establishment and will have dealings with none other. Let Mistress Betty be brought."

As soon as the little girl appeared, the young Indian, kneeling gracefully, presented her with his gift. After the tiny snow-shoes had been passed from hand to hand for inspection and their use had been explained, Lady Effingham said,—

"Now, Betty, give him the present fetched from Bristol."

Thus saying she placed a small packet in the child's hand, and the latter, advancing shyly, handed it to Nahma. With a smiling face the young warrior undid the wrappings of the packet until its contents were exposed. Suddenly his expression changed to one of consternation and bewilderment. For a moment he held the object in his hands gazing at it wildly and in evident perplexity. Then he uttered a great cry and a gush of tears filled his eyes. He gasped and seemed about to speak; but, words failing him, he turned and fled from the hall, leaving its occupants amazed at his strange actions.

"It is doubtless a native charm of some kind," quoth the knight, breaking the silence, "and a powerful one at that, for never did I see a man so upset by a trifle. After a little, when he has had time to quiet down, I will question him concerning his agitation, but until then we must amuse ourselves with conjecture."

In the mean time Nahma had not paused in his flight until reaching his own lodge. There he sat down and examined his newly acquired prize with minutest care, alternately laughing and crying as he did so. At length, apparently satisfied with his inspection, he said aloud in the long forgotten tongue of the Wampanoags,—

"Truly it is my father's wampum, and I am Nahma, the son of Longfeather."

It was indeed the Belt of Seven Totems, thus marvellously restored to him from whose unconscious form it had been taken nearly three years earlier in the far-away land of the Iroquois. Not only had Nahma thus regained his father's badge of authority, but at sight of it the memory of his earlier years, lost to him ever since he had been struck down by Miantinomo, was abruptly and fully restored. He recalled who he was and found himself once more in command of his native tongue. He also remembered every incident of his journey to the country of the Maqua as though it had been undertaken but the day before. He even remembered lying down for a brief rest after eating his supper on the western bank of the Shatemuc; but beyond that came a blank, and his next memory was of Aeana in the lodge of Kaweras.

As these things passed through his mind in rapid review, he was also whelmed by a great wave of home-sickness. The voices of his own people rang in his ears, and he heard the plash of waves on the beach at Montaup. The scent of burning cedar from the evening camp-fires was in his nostrils, and he felt the spring of brown pine needles beneath his feet as he threaded the dim forest trails of his native land. In a bark canoe he once more ran the foaming rapids of great rivers, or, lying beside Tasquanto, he was lulled to sleep by the roar of mighty cataracts. So distinct were the pictures thus flashed before him by the magic belt that he had no longer a wish to live unless he could once more gaze upon them in reality. Every other feeling was merged in an intense desire to regain his own country and rejoin his own people.

At length the longing for these things became so great that the youth sprang to his feet, determined to set forth at once in quest of them. His reason told him that such an adventure was well-nigh hopeless; but the wampum belt urged him forward and persuaded him that by some means he would succeed. So Nahma departed forever from the lodge that, but an hour earlier, had seemed his home for life, and set forth on the tremendous journey. He took with him only his weapons, a fur cloak, the fire-bag that had once belonged to Aeana, and the Belt of Seven Totems girded about his body next his skin.

As he emerged from the lodge he stood for a moment irresolute. Whither should he turn? What path would lead him to Montaup? Then the last word uttered in his hearing by Betty's mother rang again in his ears. It was "Bristol." From there the belt had but recently come, and there he would begin to retrace its mysterious course to the place where he had lost it. He had heard the foresters speak of Bristol, and he knew that it lay in the direction of the setting sun. What Bristol was, or how far away, he did not know, any more than what he should do upon getting there. It was enough that his first step was decided upon, and without a single backward glance he began his long homeward journey.

An hour later Sir Amory on his good horse Baldric, and with mistress Betty in his arms, rode up to the deserted lodge and uttered a cheery call for its supposed occupant to come forth. The knight was puzzled at finding the place empty; and for several days thereafter he caused search to be made for its recent owner. But nothing came of this, nor for many years did he hear a word concerning the disappearance and whereabouts of Massasoit.

That night Nahma slept in the wood, as lonely and friendless a human being as could be found in all the world, but so happy in his regained memory and in the knowledge that he, like others, could now lay claim to home and people, towards whom he was journeying, that nothing else mattered. On the morrow he struck the broad trail of a highway that led to the westward, and thereafter he followed it. Noting that his appearance attracted attention from the few travellers whom he met, he determined to procure a suit of clothing that would render him less conspicuous.

He dreaded to approach a house, and was at a loss how to accomplish his purpose until at dusk of the second day. Then he ran across a camp-fire surrounded by a group of dark-skinned persons, who for a moment he believed to be people of his own race. He did not discover his mistake until he was within the circle of fire-light and it was too late to retreat. So he put on a bold face, accepted an invitation to eat with the gypsies, and strove hard, though without success, to understand what they said.

They in turn were as much puzzled by him as he was by them; but this did not prevent them from exchanging a well-worn suit of clothing for Nahma's fur robe when he intimated by signs his willingness to make such a trade. As soon as he procured these things he put them on over his buckskin garments; and, as a dilapidated cap had been thrown in to complete the bargain, he was so thoroughly disguised that even Sir Amory would have failed to recognize him.

The gypsies invited their guest to cast his fortunes with them, and proposed among themselves to compel him to do so in any event. He neither declined nor accepted their offer, but after a while lay down to sleep near their fire, as though willing, at any rate, to remain with them for the present. Thus they were much chagrined to find in the morning that he had disappeared without leaving a trace to show which way he had gone.

So it happened that our wanderer came at length to the snug little seaport of Bristol, at that time second in importance only to London. And thus was taken the first step of his momentous journey. Dusk was falling as he entered the place, and for some time he wandered aimlessly through its narrow streets.

Then, unexpectedly, he came to the water front and discovered ships, some under sail and others anchored in the stream. His heart leaped at sight of them, for he supposed that all ships passed to and from his own country. Therefore if he could only find one about to depart, and contrive to get on board, the second and longest step of his journey would be provided for.

He managed to exchange his bow and arrows for a meal in a small public-house near the water, and when he had eaten it he again strolled outside looking for a place in which to pass the night. It was now quite dark, and, without going far, he lay down to sleep under the lee of a boat that was drawn up on one of the wharves.

Some hours later he was awakened by sounds of shouting and scuffling close at hand, and sprang to his feet in alarm. As he did so a rough voice called out,—

"Here's another stout fellow! Seize him, lads, and hustle him along."

Immediately Nahma was surrounded, and, despite his furious struggles, was quickly overthrown and securely bound.

CHAPTER XXV

BACK TO AMERICA

For a short space our lad was heart-broken by this rude awakening from his dreams of freedom and of a return to his own country. Half dazed as he was, he had fought desperately; and now, hustled along in company with a dozen other unfortunates, all bound and suffering from rough handling, his sole thought was of how he could soonest put an end to the life that he was resolved not to pass in slavery. He recalled with satisfaction the dirk that, hidden in his clothing, still remained to him, and was determined to use it at the earliest opportunity, first on such of his present enemies as he could reach and then on himself.

Suddenly his sombre reflections were interrupted and given a decided change of direction by finding himself crowded, together with his wretched companions, into a boat. No sooner had it received them than it was rowed out to the mouth of the harbor where stood a ship under easy sail.

From the moment of realizing that he was in a boat Nahma was filled with a wild hope, and when he was transferred from it to the deck of a waiting ship this hope was confirmed. For some reason utterly beyond his comprehension he had once more been kidnapped, but only to be placed in the very position he had longed to attain.

The ways of the white man were past understanding. Why had he been brought by force from his own country? and why should an equal amount of anxiety now be shown, and even a greater amount of force be used, to carry him back to it? He could not imagine, nor did he care. It was enough that the second step of his homeward journey had been taken for him and that the object he had so ardently desired was accomplished.

Nahma would gladly have remained on deck and attempted to make himself useful without a thought of escaping or of doing harm to those who had unwittingly so aided his plans. But this was not permitted, and he was bundled below with the poor wretches who had been ruthlessly torn from their homes to be taken as bondsmen to the Virginia plantations.

So great was the demand for labor in that colony that criminals were sent there to work out their sentences and debtors to labor until their indebtedness was discharged. In fact, all of whom society wished to rid itself were shipped across the ocean. Men anxious to try their fortunes in the New World but too poor to pay their passage went out under contract, to serve any master who would purchase their time until they had made good the money thus advanced. But even these sources of supply were not sufficient to satisfy the demand for laborers, and unscrupulous shipmasters found great profit in gathering up unsuspecting citizens by means of press-gangs sent ashore on the eve of departure, getting them on board, and sailing at once for the distant scene of their enforced servitude.

Thus Nahma now found himself in a motley company of mechanics, sailors, small tradesmen, 'prentice lads, and others, all being carried away against their will and without the knowledge of their friends. Some had left dependent families unprovided for, while others were parted from sweethearts or newly married wives. To us of to-day all this sounds incredible; but the age of "good Queen Bess" was an age of cruelty, when even the best thinking persons only shrugged their shoulders on hearing of such things, and thanked their stars that they were not in similar plight.

Some of the group now surrounding Nahma in the small space allotted to them, which was dimly lighted by a vilely smoking lamp, were groaning, some weeping, others were bemoaning their hard fate, and all were as wretchedly unhappy as it is possible for mortals to be. That is, all except our young Indian, who was overjoyed at finding himself on a ship that he believed would carry him back to his own country and people.

The kidnapped men were kept below for several days, or until land was out of sight and the ship was ploughing her slow way across the Bay of Biscay; but after that they were allowed on deck from sunrise until dark. As Nahma, buoyed by hope and eager anticipation, was the only one among them who was not seasick, he was compelled to act as steward of their mess. At first his duties in this capacity were light and he performed them willingly, but later, when his companions had gained their sea-legs, they forced all sorts of disagreeable tasks upon him, and treated him with such cruelty that his hatred of white men was increased a hundred-fold.

They were much puzzled over his nationality, which he never revealed, though often questioned concerning it. Most of them declared that he was a gypsy, while others insisted that he was of negro blood and called him "Guinea." The captain of the ship while strongly suspecting him to be an American would not admit it, but spoke of him as a "Jack Spaniard."

So slow was the weary voyage that it was two months to a day before the westerly winds against which they were beating brought to Nahma's sensitive nostrils the first scent of land. That evening he hid himself on deck so that he might sniff the air all night, and at daybreak he was rewarded by the sight of land lying cloud-like on the western horizon.

During that day he was so inattentive to his enforced duties as to win many a blow and kick from his brutal masters. Although the young Indian's blood boiled with rage, he did not attempt to resent these things, but submitted to them with an assumed meekness that ill-expressed his feelings. He felt that he could afford to abide his time, for was he not almost within reach of his own people? At the same time deep down in his heart he vowed a bitter vengeance against those who thus degraded him, if ever the opportunity should come. And it came sooner than he expected, though not through his own people, as he had hoped.

Before the features of the landfall became recognizable the wind hauled to the eastward and the weather thickened, with every indication of a storm. Thus the skipper was greatly relieved shortly before night to find his ship running into a broad bay between two distant headlands that he believed to be the capes of Virginia, though in reality they were those of Delaware. Without attempting to discover the mouth of the James, he sought only a lee under which the night might be passed in safety.

When this was found and the ship was snugly anchored for the first time since leaving Bristol, not only the captain but his entire company began a carouse to celebrate this successful termination of their perilous voyage. Liquor flowed freely in the cabin, and was served forward in such generous measure that a liberal portion even found its way to the wretched bondmen who expected shortly to be sold into years of servitude. Thus by midnight nearly every man on board was helplessly drunk, and most of them were asleep.

Up to this hour the storm had steadily increased in violence, and the ship, though still safe, was surging heavily at her cables. At the same time but a single figure was in motion on her decks, and he was creeping forward as stealthily as though fearful of being discovered. Gaining the bow undetected, he bent for a minute over one of the straining cables, and when he arose two of its hempen strands had been severed. Then he stepped quickly to the other, drew his keen blade across it once, twice, three times, and with the last stroke it parted. The one first cut gave way almost at the same moment, and the freed ship started up the bay like a restive steed just given a loose rein.

With his long-meditated design thus successfully accomplished, Nahma darted back to his place of hiding and awaited developments. He had long since discovered that he was destined to be sold into slavery among those white men who had settled far to the southward of his own country. Tales of their injustice and cruelty towards the natives had reached Montaup even before he left there, and had filled his boyish heart with a fierce indignation. Now he was determined not to fall alive into their hands, and believed that on this night or never he must effect an escape. He could not swim to shore because of the distance and the heavy seas. All the ship's boats were inboard and securely lashed, so that he could not make off in one of them. Consequently his only feasible plan seemed to be to let the ship herself drift until she fetched up on some beach, from which he might gain the safe cover of the woods. He had never experienced a shipwreck and knew nothing of its terrors. Even if he had he would not have hesitated to carry out his desperate plan.

The captain of the drifting ship, too hard-headed to be overcome by any amount of liquor, was the first to become aware that her cables had parted. He stumbled on deck, bawling out orders that were mingled with strange oaths, and, gaining the wheel, put his vessel's head before the wind that she might scud without danger of being thrown on her beam ends. Then he bellowed for assistance, but it came tardily, and was of slight avail. There was but one spare anchor, and when finally it was broken out, bent on, and got overboard, the ship was so far in the open that it could not hold.

So the helpless vessel drifted for several hours, and shortly before day-break struck with such force that all of her masts went by the board. Then ensued a period of horrible crashing, grinding, and pounding, with which were mingled the shrieks of drowning men. Some of the strongest swimmers reached the shore, bruised and breathless but still alive, and foremost among them was the almost naked form of him who had caused the disaster.

Battered and beaten by roaring breakers, weak and nearly perished with cold, Nahma was at the same time upheld by such a spirit of exultation as he had never before known. He was once more free and once more lying on the beloved soil of his native land. No sooner had he regained his breath after being flung on the beach than he struggled to his feet and staggered to the safe shelter of a forest that grew almost to the water's edge. He did not look back nor give a thought to what was taking place behind him. The white men who would have sold him into slavery might care for themselves, as might those who had so recently degraded him by their blows and curses.

An hour later our young Indian was seated by a camp-fire of the Saga-naga or Delawares, and telling them in sign language, supplemented by the few words they had in common, of the wonderful treasure that the sea had brought to their very doors.

They, recognizing the splendid belt of wampum that he wore, listened to him with closest attention; and when he had finished, all the able-bodied men of the village hastened to the scene of the wreck, leaving Nahma to the kindly hospitality of those who remained behind.

That night there was no village in the Delaware nation, nor probably on the entire Atlantic coast, so rich in scalps and plunder as the one in which the son of Longfeather was an honored guest.

CHAPTER XXVI

SASSACUS THE PEQUOT

This utter destruction of the ship and of her entire company gave great satisfaction not only to the young Indian who had suffered so much on her but to the Saganaga, who were at that time feeling very bitter against white men on account of the recent stealing of a number of their tribe to be sold into slavery. It had been the usual case of a cordial welcome to the strangers from beyond the sea, a brisk trade by which the confidence of the Indians was won, and then a sudden sailing with some twenty of them on board. Now, thanks to Nahma, the Lenni Lenape were revenged and their hearts were lightened of a burden.

Also they had acquired wealth beyond their wildest dreams, and were very grateful to him who had thrown it in their way. He did not tell them that he had been a slave in the white man's country, for he was determined to keep that humiliating knowledge to himself. So he only gave them to understand that he too had been kidnapped, and let them imagine it to have been of recent occurrence.

They had at once recognized the Belt of Seven Totems that Nahma wore diagonally across his breast when first appearing among them, though no member of their tribe had ever before seen it. They, however, knew it from description; for, among American Indians, tribal totems and the belts of principal chieftains were as well known as are the banners of European nations, and the coats of arms of their rulers, among white men. The Saganaga also knew that none but Longfeather or his eldest son might wear the Belt of Seven Totems, and so they treated Nahma with every mark of consideration.

Finding that he was desirous of returning at once to his own country, they furnished him with clothing, weapons, and a belt of wampum bearing the likeness of a serpent, which he was to deliver to the Peacemaker as a badge of friendship. They also provided an escort of young warriors, who would guide him to the country of the Pavonias. These people, who were a branch of the Saganaga, occupied the territory lying on the south side of the Shatemuc at the point where it flows into the sea, and they willingly furnished Nahma with a canoe in which to continue his journey.

Launching this craft on the waters of the narrow, tide-swept channel afterwards known as the Kill von Kull, and receiving from his friends a goodly store of parched corn, our traveller set forth alone on the last stage of his homeward journey.

On leaving the Kill he crossed New York Bay, undotted by a single sail, passed the densely wooded island that was to be known as "Governor's," and entered the East River. Here he came upon a scene of enchanting beauty. On his right stretched the level salt marshes and wooded plains of Long Island. On the other hand lay rock-ribbed Manhattan, rugged with hills and valleys, among which sparkled many crystal springs and rippling brooks. It was covered from end to end and from water's edge to water's edge with groves of stately forest-trees interspersed with grassy glades in which fed herds of deer. Over all was flung the exquisite veil of a May verdure, while the air was heavy with the scent of blossoms and filled with the song of mating birds. On the river's edge brown rocks were fringed with fantastic sea-growths that waved in the swift tide like banners streaming in a breeze.

Brooding ducks and wading heron peopled every placid cove, fish leaped from the clear waters, and white-plumed gulls flecked the blue sky. The beauty and peace of nature reigned undisturbed over all; for, as yet, no Old World keel had cleaved those waters, and the site of what was destined to become the greatest city of the earth was still untainted by the blight of civilization. Nor did Nahma see a human being on his whole journey from bay to sound. In the place destined to hold millions of his kind he was alone.

Skirting the northern shore of Long Island Sound, the solitary voyager, always taking pains to avoid observation, passed the country of the Mohicans and entered upon that of the Pequots. During the four days thus occupied he had not held communication with any man, having shunned alike the infrequent villages of bark huts and the camp-fires of fishermen or shell gatherers, as well as their canoes. He did not wish to be delayed or recognized before reaching the country of his own people. Consequently he hesitated for a moment when, on the fourth day of his journey, he discovered two figures in a canoe making signals of distress.

They were midway between an island lying several miles off shore and the mainland, and their canoe was so low in the water that it seemed about to sink. One of the figures was that of a man, who was paddling with desperate energy, while the other, evidently a woman, was furiously bailing water from the sinking craft. Only for a moment did Nahma hesitate, and then he headed with all speed in that direction.

The water-logged canoe sank before he reached it; but, within a few minutes, he had rescued the survivors, and they were safely bestowed in his own craft. With this accomplished, he started towards the land that had been their objective-point when, as he afterwards learned, their canoe had been pierced and ripped open by a sword-fish. Whether this had been done with malice, playfully, or by accident they could not tell; but it had so endangered their lives that they would, almost of a certainty, have drowned had not the stranger come to their rescue.

Not a word was spoken by any one of the three until the canoe had nearly gained the land. Then the rescued man, who, though young, was of commanding aspect, turned from his paddling in the bow and said,—

"Thou hast saved us from death and I will not forget it. I am Sassacus, chief of the Pequots."

Nahma's heart leaped within him. The Pequots formed one of the tribes acknowledging the authority of his father, and this youth was his own cousin. He was about to make reply, when the other continued: "I perceive thou art a stranger, and if thy business be not too pressing, my lodge would be honored to shelter thee as a guest."

"Gladly would I tarry," was the reply, "but I may not, for I bear a belt from the Saganaga to Longfeather the Peacemaker, that must be promptly delivered. The name by which I am known is Massasoit."

The Pequot chieftain turned and gazed keenly at the speaker. "Have not the Lenni Lenape learned that Longfeather has gone the great journey?" he asked.

"Dead! Longfeather dead, and I not with him at the end!" cried Nahma, shocked by the suddenness of this news into an unpremeditated betrayal of feeling. "When did he die, and how? Was he killed in battle?"

"He went to the place of Okis when the willow leaves were the size of mouse-ears, and he was killed by the pale-faces who come from the sea with death and destruction in their hands," answered the young chieftain, bitterly.

"Killed by the white man!" gasped Nahma, his face growing black and the cords of his neck swelling with rage. "Then by his blood I swear——"

"Wait," commanded Sassacus. "Not directly did the men from the sea take his life, nor was his blood shed. With the falling of leaves one of their winged canoes came to land near Montaup. From it were set on shore two men more nearly dead than living. Then the great canoe departed, leaving them to die. The dwellers of that country took pity on them and cared for them; but they died, and in a short time all who had gone near them were also dead. The plague spread from the Pokanokets to the Nausets, the Nipmucks, the Naticks, the Abenakis, and may still be spreading in the land of cold, though on this side it was stayed by the coming of warm weather, and thy—— Longfeather was the last to die of it."

For a few moments Nahma sat silent. Then, lifting his face, on which were unconcealed traces of a mighty grief, he said, "I will go with thee, Sassacus."

"It is well," replied the other, and no further word was spoken between them until after a landing was made. Even then the subject that had so greatly affected the new-comer was not again mentioned until after he had been taken to the lodge of the young chieftain and refreshed. This having been done, the guest requested that his host would walk apart with him, and when they were by themselves he said,—

"Thy news of the Peacemaker hath so confused my plans that I am at a loss how to proceed and would learn further from thee. First I would know who exercises authority in place of the great Wampanoag? Left he a son to rule in his stead?"

Sassacus looked curiously at his guest as he answered,—

"Longfeather had a son who should take his place, but he disappeared many moons ago."

"How?"

"No man knows for a certainty. Some say that he joined the Iroquois, and others that he was taken prisoner by the Hurons of the cold land. In that case there is small chance of his being now alive."

"Who, then, wears the Belt of Seven Totems?"

"No one wears it," replied the other, gravely, "for it also disappeared at the same time. Miantinomo the Narragansett claims the place and authority of Longfeather in the name of Canonicus, his father, and is even now at Montaup."

"Miantinomo!" exclaimed Nahma, bitterly. "By what right does he make such a claim?"

"By the right of a strong arm," replied the other.

"Is he loved and respected as was Longfeather?"

"No; he is hated by many and feared by all."

"Why, then, was he allowed to assume authority?"

"Because there was none other to dispute him."

"If one should come——?" began Nahma, hesitatingly.

"If one should come wearing the Belt of Seven Totems, or bearing other proof that he is the son of Longfeather," said Sassacus quickly, and with a meaning glance at his companion, "then would he find many to support his claim."

For a full minute Nahma hesitated, and the young men gazed steadfastly at each other. Then Nahma slowly thrust a hand within his buckskin shirt, and, drawing forth the Belt of Seven Totems, displayed it to his companion.

"Here is the Peacemaker's badge of authority," he said, "and here also is he who should succeed him, for I am Nahma, son of Longfeather."

"I have known it, my brother," replied Sassacus, "since the moment I saw thy face on hearing news of thy father's death, but I would not speak till thou hadst spoken. Now, however, I gladly acknowledge thee as my sachem, and will at once make public announcement of thy coming."

"Not so," objected Nahma. "For the present, and until I can meet Miantinomo face to face, I must be Massasoit of the Lenni Lenape. If, however, my brother will go to Montaup with a following of his young men, I will gladly travel in his company."

CHAPTER XXVII

A ROYAL HOME-COMING

By murder, treachery, fraud, and force Miantinomo the Narragansett had finally attained the position upon which he had so long cast envious eyes. At the death of Longfeather he had caused himself to be proclaimed Peacemaker, or ruler of the confederated New England tribes, in the name of his adopted father, who was now too old to take an active part in affairs of this kind. The various stories concerning Nahma, circulated from time to time, had not disturbed him, for did he not know that his rival was dead? Nor had he any fear that the Belt of Seven Totems would ever again be seen in those parts, since he had given it to a white trader in exchange for a hatchet, and it had been carried to that mysterious place beyond the sea from which nothing ever returned.

He had also learned with satisfaction of Sacandaga's death, for that chieftain was the only red man who had ever seen the belt in his possession. With all traces of his own treacherous dealings thus wiped out, the ambitious young man had no hesitation in proclaiming Canonicus, his father, to be Longfeather's successor by virtue of his position as head of the strongest tribe in the confederation.

Although Miantinomo was generally disliked, no person felt strong enough to dispute this claim, and so he was sullenly accepted as Lawgiver of the tribes. In this capacity he hastened to take possession of Montaup, which had become the recognized seat of government.

There he at once proceeded to belie his assumed character of Peacemaker by making preparations on a large scale for invading the country of the Iroquois. He had never forgiven them for refusing to treat with him simply as a Narragansett, and now that he was in a position to command a war-party equal to any they could put in the field, he believed the time for humiliating them had come. He sent a runner to the Hurons urging them to attack the Iroquois from the north about the time that he proposed to cross the Shatemuc, and he imagined that the combination thus formed would prove overpowering. He also hoped that all this warlike activity would divert the thoughts of those who were displeased with his usurpation of authority, and he knew that a successful war would firmly establish his position.

So Miantinomo had sent messengers to every tribe and clan of the New England Confederacy bidding their warriors assemble at Montaup, and already were a great number thus gathered. Among others Sassacus had received a summons to this effect, but the fiery Pequot had determined to disobey it and risk the consequences. Now, however, the coming of Nahma had so changed the aspect of affairs that he gladly accepted the invitation to present himself at Montaup accompanied by a strong body of picked warriors.

Miantinomo, who had feared that Sassacus more than any other might rebel against his self-assumed authority, received him with effusive hospitality.

"Now do I know," he said, "that my undertaking against the arrogant Iroquois will succeed, since they have no warriors to equal the Pequots in bravery."

"It is good that you esteem my young men so highly," replied Sassacus, "and it is certain that they will do what may be to establish firmly the power of the Peacemaker. I am also accompanied to Montaup by one who will doubtless prove more welcome than all the others. He is a medicine-man of the Saganaga, who brings to the Peacemaker a belt of friendship from his people."

"Say you so!" exclaimed Miantinomo, his dark face lighting with pleasure, for an alliance with the Lenni Lenape of the south as well as one with the Hurons of the north would render him invincible. "Where is he? Why has he not already been brought to the lodge of council?"

"He is an old man and weary, who secludes himself from the common gaze in a lodge of skins that was pitched for him as soon as the canoes came to land," replied Sassacus. "He desires not to make his message public, since it is for your ears alone. For this reason he requests that a new medicine-lodge be erected in which he may receive you in private and with ceremonies befitting so important an occasion."

"An old man say you?" inquired Miantinomo, doubtfully.

"He has every appearance of extreme age and decrepitude."

"Have you seen the belt that he bears?"

"I have seen it, and know it to be a serpent-belt of the Saganaga. He hopes also to take one from you, that his people may know his mission to have been truly performed. If his terms be not granted, then with his belt will he depart to the land of the Iroquois."

"Without doubt I will grant all that he asks," replied Miantinomo, hastily, "for a friendship with the Saganaga may not be thrown away. At once shall a medicine-lodge be built, and when next the shadows are shortest then will I meet him."

"If it is your pleasure I will see to the building of the lodge," said Sassacus.

"It is my pleasure," answered the other, and with this the interview ended.

By noon of the following day the medicine-lodge, a simple affair of poles and bark, stood finished on the edge of a cleared space that formed the public gathering-place of Montaup. It was a mere shell bare of all furnishings, as was noted by the many curious persons who peeped in at its open doorway. The news that something of absorbing interest was to take place within it had attracted a large assemblage to its vicinity, where they waited with eager curiosity.

At the same time there was but little mingling of those belonging to the several tribes represented. The Narragansetts, with Miantinomo seated in front of them, were grouped by themselves close to the lodge but a little to one side. Although they outnumbered any of the visiting delegations, they formed but a fraction of the whole gathering.

Opposite to them and equally near the lodge stood the Pequots with the plumed head of Sassacus towering above them, and beside him stood our old acquaintance, Samoset.

The Wampanoags were there in full force supported by a large delegation of their near relatives, the Pokanokets. Besides these were representatives of every New England tribe that had acknowledged the authority of Longfeather. All were warriors, armed as for battle, and headed by their most experienced chiefs.

About half an hour before the sun attained his meridian a distant chanting of voices, accompanied by the measured beating of medicine-drums, announced the opening of the ceremonies, and a buzz of expectation swept over the great assembly.

Then appeared a procession of medicine-men clad in fantastic garb calculated to inspire those who beheld it with awe. Most prominent among them was an old man enveloped in a long robe of costly furs. He was so feeble and bent with age that he leaned heavily upon a stick and was also supported by two attendants. Directly in front of him walked a boy, very proud of his honorable position, and bearing in outstretched hands the wampum serpent-belt of the Saganaga so displayed that all might see it.

The procession halted before the lodge, while its members engaged in a medicine-dance, circling with furious gestures and wild cries about the central figure of the old man. Precisely at the hour of noon the dancing came to an abrupt end, and the old medicine-man, taking from the boy who had borne it the belt of the Saganaga, entered the empty lodge alone.

For a few minutes his voice was heard in the feeble chanting of an incantation, and then it invited the presence of the Peacemaker. Upon this Miantinomo stepped forth without hesitation and entered the lodge, vanishing from sight beyond its heavy curtain of double deer-skins. The light of the interior was so dim that for a moment he could see nothing; then he made out the form of its solitary occupant standing before him, and holding the belt that he believed was to confirm him in his assumed position. The old man, leaning on his stick, was still enveloped in the long robe that covered him from head to foot.

Gazing steadfastly at Miantinomo, he said, sternly,—

"Why dost thou come here? I summoned Longfeather the Peacemaker."

"He is dead," replied the other, "and I——"

"Then should his son Nahma have come in his place," interrupted the old man.

"He, too, is dead," said Miantinomo; "that is," he added, hastily, "he is dead to this people, for he is a traitor and dwells in the lodges of their enemies."

"Thou, then, art authorized to fill his place?"

"I am so authorized by Canonicus, my father, and will seek to wipe out the shame cast upon the name of Longfeather by his unworthy son."

"Why, then, dost thou not wear the Peacemaker's badge of authority, the great Belt of Seven Totems?"

"Because it was stolen and carried away by Nahma the renegade."

"Now do I know that thou liest!" exclaimed the old man with an energy of voice as startling as it was unexpected. "Thou knowest, better than any other, that the son of Longfeather was foully murdered while he slept on the farther bank of the Shatemuc. Thou knowest that his body, stripped of its badge of authority, was flung into the river. Thou knowest that the Belt of Seven Totems, first used to blind the eyes of Sacandaga, was afterwards sold to a white-faced trader that it might disappear forever beyond the salt waters. Thou knowest who first put in circulation the false tale that the son of Longfeather was a traitor and a renegade. Thou knowest, and I know, for such things may not be hid from the Okis. Also will I prove to thee that the dead may live, and that evil designs may come to naught even when they seem most likely to succeed. Look, then, and tremble, thou dog of a murderer."

With these words the dimly outlined form of the old man straightened into erectness, his stick fell to the ground, he flung back his enveloping robe, and at the same moment a slab of bark dropped from the roof of the lodge, allowing a flood of noonday sunlight to stream on the place where he stood.

For an instant Miantinomo stared dumbly at the figure, young, tall, and handsome, richly clad and wearing across its breast the Peacemaker's Belt of Seven Totems, that gazed sternly at him with accusing eyes. Then, with a great cry of terror, he rushed from the lodge and fled like one who is pursued by a deadly vengeance in the direction of the nearest forest.

As the startled assemblage, gathered to witness his crowning triumph, gazed after the flying figure in bewilderment, their attention was further attracted, and they were thrilled by a shout of joyful amaze. Instantly all eyes were again turned towards the lodge, where in place of an old medicine-man stood a young chieftain, as noble a specimen of his race as ever trod American soil. Depending from one shoulder was the long-lost Belt of Seven Totems and from the other a serpent-belt of the Saganaga. At his feet knelt Samoset, crying out that it was indeed his brother and his master, Nahma, the son of Longfeather.

"I am the son of Longfeather, and I was Nahma," said the young man, so distinctly that all might hear. "But now and henceforth am I Massasoit the Peacemaker."

Upon this the whole assemblage, led by Sassacus and his loyal Pequots, broke into a joyous tumult of welcome and crowded about the youth who, so long lost to them, had been thus marvellously restored to his rightful position. Only the Narragansetts took advantage of the glad confusion to steal away unnoticed and follow the trail of their dishonored leader.

CHAPTER XXVIII

IN THE COUNCIL-LODGE

Massasoit could not relate the whole story of his adventurous wanderings, since no Indian known to have been a slave might afterwards be accepted as a leader among his people. Consequently he omitted all reference to his unhappy experiences in England. Nor did he ever mention that he had crossed the great salt waters; but he told of his adventures among the Iroquois, as a captive to the Hurons, while in Quebec, and on a ship that was to have carried him into slavery among the Yengeese of the south. He described the destruction of that ill-fated craft, together with the loss of her company, his own welcome at the hands of the Saganaga, and his homeward journey, to all of which the assemblage listened with breathless attention. In conclusion, the young chieftain said,—

"I have told all there is to tell. When I left you Longfeather ruled this land. He has gone from you never to return. I am his son, and it was his wish that I should be Peacemaker in his place. If that be also your desire, or if it be not, now is the time to speak. Will you have Massasoit for your sagamore or another?"

Standing very straight and gazing proudly about him, the young man awaited an answer, and it was promptly given. First came Sassacus, saying,—

"The Pequots accept Massasoit as their Peacemaker and will listen to his words."

After him in grave procession came the chiefs to tender their allegiance; and a few days later the venerable Canonicus came also, for Massasoit had not told that Miantinomo had attempted to murder him, and so the Narragansetts were not yet outcast from the federation.

Thus did Massasoit occupy his father's place in the great lodge of council, while his authority was acknowledged from the Shatemuc to the sea, and from the country of the Mohicans to that of the Hurons, who dwelt near the great river of the north.

With his position thus established, the young sachem, leaving Sassacus to hold Montaup during his absence, set forth on an expedition of the utmost importance both to himself and to his people. It had three objects: first, to find his mother, who had fled from Miantinomo; second, to restore the peaceful relations with the Iroquois that had been threatened by the usurper; and last, but by no means least, to visit the lodge of Kaweras.

As a following worthy of his rank he took with him one hundred warriors, and with these he pressed forward over the trail that he had followed as a youth three years earlier. At the village of Peace, on the river of sweet waters, he found Miantomet, and raised her in a moment from the dejection of a childless fugitive to a proud motherhood, with the son, whom she had so long mourned as dead, once more restored to her.

But only for a short time might these two enjoy their reunion, for Massasoit found that whole section of country alarmed over an invasion of Hurons, who were said to be coming down the valley of the Shatemuc in formidable numbers. So he pushed on, hoping to form a junction with the Iroquois before the common enemy should arrive.

The eastern Iroquois or Maquas were hard beset. Two powerful expeditions had descended at once upon the country of the Five Nations. One, under leadership of our old acquaintance Champlain, had crossed Lake Ontario, penetrated deep into the territory of the Oneidas, and was supposed to be advancing upon the Maquas from the west. Another expedition, accompanied by three white men, was coming from the north by way of the Shatemuc, and already were fugitives flying before them to the palisaded villages, bringing sad tales of rapine and destruction. As though this state of affairs were not bad enough, it was reported that the New England tribes, led by Miantinomo, were advancing from the east. Thus it seemed as though the Maquas were doomed to destruction, and a feeling of despair had seized upon the warriors gathered for the defence of their three palisaded strongholds.

One night, during this unhappy condition of suspense, a group of chief men were seated about a small fire in the council-house of the easternmost village, gloomily discussing the situation. News had come that the enemy was close at hand, and that the village would be assaulted by overwhelming numbers on the morrow. So oppressed were the councillors by the hopelessness of their situation that for some time they sat in silence, and one among them appeared to be dozing, as though exhausted.

Suddenly this one, who was our old friend Kaweras, awoke, uttering an exclamation of pleasure, and looked about him with smiling cheerfulness.

"What pleases my brother?" asked he who sat nearest. "Has he seen a vision of the spirit land to which all of us will go before the setting of another sun?"

"No," replied Kaweras. "It is not yet time for visions of the spirit land."

"How so, when even the youngest warrior knows that we are in no condition to withstand an attack of the Hurons and of those armed with thundersticks who accompany them?"

"It is because he who is to deliver us even now approaches, and in a vision have I seen him."

"Comes he from the west, and is he the Wild-Cat of the Oneidas?"

"No. He is from the east, and more powerful than the Wild-Cat or any other single chieftain of the Iroquois. He is not of us, but he has already fought with us. I have known him, but until now I have not known him. Whence he comes or how he has passed our young men I know not, but even now he is at hand. Behold, he is here!"

The old man had risen to his feet in his excitement, and now stood staring eagerly at the skin-hung entrance.

As he finished speaking the curtain was drawn aside and a young warrior stepped within the lodge. He advanced to where the firelight fell full upon his face, and then stood motionless as though awaiting recognition. Nor was it long in coming, for, after a moment of silence, Kaweras stepped forward with extended hand, uttering the single word, "Massasoit."

"Yes, my father, it is Massasoit," was the reply; but the old man hardly noticed what was said, for his eye had fallen on a belt worn by the newcomer, and he was studying its devices with an expression of amazement. Finally he said, in a low tone,—

"It is the Belt of Seven Totems, the great colier of the Peacemaker."

"And I," responded Massasoit, "am the Peacemaker, since I was Nahma, son of Longfeather. For thy exceeding kindness to me in other days am I now come with a war-party to help the people of Sacandaga in their time of trouble."

"How came he inside our walls?" asked one of the chiefs, suspiciously.

"That will I tell at another time," replied Massasoit. "Now there are things of more importance to be considered."

The young man did not care to acknowledge that Aeana had given him admittance, but so it was. He had left his warriors in concealment at some distance from the village while he went alone to discover the exact state of affairs.

That same afternoon, before warning of the near approach of the Hurons had been given, he had seen several women go to a small stream for water, and recognized Aeana among them. After a while he managed to toss a small packet so that it fell at her feet. Glancing about with a startled air, the girl picked it up, and found in it the embroidered tinder-bag that she had concealed in her sister's gift to Massasoit so long ago that she had almost forgotten the incident. As she gazed at the token, hardly knowing whether to be frightened or pleased, the low call of a wood-dove attracted her attention to a nearby thicket. Hesitatingly she moved close enough to hear the whispered words, "Be not afraid. I am here as a friend to help the Maquas against their enemies; but first I would see Kaweras. At moon-setting will I come alone to the gate, and I rely upon thee to give me admittance."

Outwardly calm, but with a wildly fluttering heart, Aeana rejoined her companions without having been for an instant out of their sight, and returned with them to the village. There she debated long with herself as to whether she should tell her father or Otshata of what had happened; but, until the time of moon-setting, she had not found courage to do so. She had not meant to admit the young warrior without their knowledge, especially as news had come, within an hour, of the near approach of the Hurons; but a will stronger than her own seemed to compel her, and finally she did as Massasoit desired. Then, sadly frightened, she whispered, "In the council-house is Kaweras," and fled away into the darkness, leaving the young man to discover his bearings as best he might.

Having at length gained the council-lodge and being received as already stated, Massasoit was compelled to answer many questions before securing the confidence of all the chiefs. Little by little, however, it was acquired. Kaweras told what he knew of him. The belt that he wore was a potent influence; and finally one, who had been with Sacandaga at the time of his death, recognized the young man as he who had risked his own life to save that of the Iroquois chieftain. After that they listened with closest attention to all he had to say. Thus, before he left them, he had outlined a plan of operations for the morrow, or whenever the Hurons should make an attack, that they promised to follow.

Massasoit also instructed the Iroquois as to the nature of fire-arms, which they had heretofore regarded with all the terror of ignorance. He described the manner in which the thunder-sticks must be loaded before becoming effective as weapons, and assured his hearers that, after being discharged, they were for a long time no more dangerous than so many wooden billets. Having thus restored a cheerful confidence to the council, the young chieftain departed and made his way to where his own warriors anxiously awaited him.

Immediately upon rejoining these, and without pausing to rest, he led them on a long detour, so that, before daylight, they had gained a position in the rear of the Hurons, by whom the presence of the young Peacemaker was as yet unsuspected.

With the rising of the sun hundreds of dark forms might have been seen gliding stealthily from tree to tree in the direction of the Maqua village. At a short interval behind the last of these came another group moving in the same direction, but with even greater caution. Foremost among them was Massasoit, leading his people in an enterprise that would make or mar his own reputation for all future time.

Suddenly the morning stillness of the forest was rudely broken by the roar of three muskets fired in quick succession, and the battle was begun.

CHAPTER XXIX

WINNING A BATTLE, A WIFE, AND A FRIEND

Upon the advice of Massasoit, the Iroquois had set up dummies to draw the musket-fire of the enemy; also most of their young men had been placed in ambush outside the walls. These, though few in number as compared with the advancing host of Hurons, sprang to their feet with frightful yells and rushed towards the place marked by the smoke of the now empty muskets. They seemed doomed to certain destruction, and the Hurons calmly awaited their coming. All at once, and without warning, a flight of arrows from the rear brought a score of the invaders to the ground, and at the same moment the woods behind them seemed alive with yelling foemen.

For a few minutes the bewildered Hurons, thus entrapped, fought desperately. Then the three white men, who were objects of Massasoit's especial vengeance, were killed while hurriedly endeavoring to reload their muskets. As they fell their savage allies, who had until now regarded them as invincible, broke into a panic-stricken flight, each man endeavoring only to save himself. After them raced Massasoit and his warriors, together with the jubilant Iroquois, and many and fierce were the hand-to-hand conflicts that took place in the dim forest coverts that day. At its close, when the wearied but exultant victors gathered once more at the wildly rejoicing village, their trophies of scalps and prisoners outnumbered their combined forces.

The following week was devoted to the wildest forms of savage festivity, and the rejoicings were redoubled near its close by the arrival of a runner from the west, bringing the great news that the other invading force under Champlain had been defeated and driven back by the Onondagas and Oneidas.

In all this time of feasting Massasoit was the hero and central figure. Not only had he saved the Maqua village and probably the whole tribe from destruction, but, on that day of fighting, he had proved himself the foremost warrior of his people and had brought in more Huron scalps than any other.

He found no difficulty in forming a compact with the Iroquois on behalf of his own people, by which both were bound not to cross the Shatemuc except for friendly visits. Thus our young chieftain would have been supremely happy but for one thing, and that was his treatment at the hands of Aeana.

This girl, who now seemed the most beautiful and desirable of all earthly creatures, behaved to him in a manner so strange that he could in no wise account for it. Not only did she refuse to grant him an interview, but she studiously avoided meeting him, and went no longer with the other women to the stream for water. Thus he had not been able to exchange a single word with her, and as the time for his departure drew near he was in despair. In his distress he sought out Otshata, as he had done once before, and, pouring out his heart, asked her what he should do.

Otshata laughed in his face. "What fools men be!" she said. "Dost thou not remember, Massasoit, the time when she bade thee fetch water?"

"Well do I remember."

"And thou performed the service?"

"Truly, I did, even as she bade me."

"And she scorned the offering when it was brought to her?"

"Even so, and taunted me with the name of 'squaw.'"

"Remembering that, art thou still at a loss to know why she now refuses to meet thee?"

"To my confusion, I am," replied the puzzled youth.

At this Otshata laughed again long and heartily; but at length she asked,—

"Didst thou ever know a woman to accept friendship with a slave when a master might be had?"

Then, still laughing, she ran away, leaving the young man to ponder her words.

As a result of this conversation, Massasoit announced that he and his warriors would depart for their own country on the morrow, and at daylight of the next morning they had disappeared. That day Aeana, heavy-hearted and with lagging step, went with the other women for water. As she bent over the stream an exclamation from one of her companions caused her to look up and directly into the eyes of Massasoit, who stood on the opposite bank.

With a shrill cry of dismay, Aeana turned and fled towards the village; but, swiftly as she ran, Massasoit overtook her ere she had covered half the distance. Seizing her in his arms, he picked her up and, despite her struggles, bore her swiftly away. On the edge of the wood he paused to utter a far-carrying yell of triumph, and then, still bearing his precious burden, he disappeared amid the leafy shadows.

But his defiant challenge was answered, and half a dozen young Iroquois, all of whom were aspirants for the hand of the arrow-maker's beautiful daughter, dashed forth in hot pursuit. This race for a bride was over a forest course something more than a mile in length. At its farther end was the Shatemuc and a waiting canoe containing a single occupant. As Massasoit gained this and it was shoved off, the foremost of his pursuers was so close that he fell into the water in a vain effort to grasp the elusive craft.

Beyond the river the Iroquois might not pass by the terms of their recent treaty, and thus on its farther side, Massasoit felt his prize to be as secure as though he already had her at Montaup.

As they stepped out on the land that acknowledged the son of Long-feather to be its ruler, Aeana regarded the bold youth with eyes that laughed even through their tears, and said, "I hate you; but if you had not done it, then should I have despised you forever."

So Massasoit won his bride, and in far-away Montaup, beside the great salt waters that bathe the rising sun, no woman led a happier life than did the daughter of Kaweras.

After this several years were passed in peaceful content by those New England tribes owning the rule of Massasoit. With his superior knowledge of the world he was able to teach them many things that caused them to prosper as never before. Only was he worried by the Narragansetts, who, while sullenly admitting his authority, awaited eagerly an opportunity to renounce and defy it.

In the mean time Aeana had presented the Peacemaker with two sons, the younger of whom, named Metacomet, was to become famous in after-years as King Philip.

With all his peace and apparent security Massasoit had one ever-present fear, and it was of the white man. He had a knowledge greater than any of his people concerning the number and power of these dwellers beyond the sea, and he dreaded lest they should seek to obtain a foothold in his country, as they had already done both on the St. Lawrence and the James. As one measure of precaution against this he issued orders to every New England tribe that they should hold no intercourse with any whites attempting to trade on the coast. So determined was he to carry out this policy that when an unfortunate French trading vessel was wrecked on a shore of Massachusetts Bay, he caused her to be burned, and commanded that all survivors of her crew be put to death.

Holding these views, Massasoit became very angry when it was reported to him that the Narragansetts, in defiance of his authority, were actively trading with an English ship that had appeared on their coast, and he at once determined to make an example that should be remembered.

A runner was despatched to his trusted ally Sassacus, whose country lay beyond that of the Narragansetts, ordering the Pequots to advance from the west until they should meet Massasoit coming from the opposite direction. Then, gathering a strong force from the tribes near at hand, the Peacemaker set forth for the scene of unlawful trading.

So demoralized were the Narragansetts by the simultaneous appearance of two powerful war-parties within their borders that they offered only a slight resistance before fleeing to their palisaded stronghold, where they anxiously awaited the expected attack.

In the mean time the captain of the English vessel, which was snugly anchored in the mouth of a small river, where he had been carrying on a brisk and most profitable trade with the Indians, was disgusted to have it suddenly cease. For days a fleet of canoes had surrounded his ship. Now not one was to be seen, nor could any of the natives be discovered on shore. His recent great success had been largely due to the fact that he had on board an English-speaking Indian, through whom all negotiations had been conducted. When a whole day had passed without change in the situation the captain consulted with this Indian, and asked what he supposed had become of the natives.

"They be fearful to come off since they have learn that you steal red men for slaves," was the answer.

"Ho, ho! Is that all? But think you, Squanto, that they have any furs left?"

"Me think they keep back many of the best."

"By the Lord Harry! Then must we go to them, since they are afraid to come to us. Boat away, there! And, Squanto, you may come too if you will promise to make no attempt at escape."

"These be not my people," replied the Indian, evasively.

"That's so. I picked you up at a great distance from here. But never mind. If you serve me truly perhaps I will take you back there some day. Attempt to play me false, though, and I will kill you as I would a rat. Tumble in, then, and let us hie ashore."

It was a strong boat's crew and heavily armed that thus made a landing in search of the trade which no longer came to their ship, and they followed a plainly marked trail leading from the beach to the place where had been an Indian village. Now it was deserted and void of life, though their guide announced that it had been occupied as recently as a few hours before.

While the new-comers were prowling about with hopes of discovering something in the way of plunder, their attention was distracted by a column of smoke rising in the direction of their boat. They had left it hauled partially out of the water and in charge of two well-armed men. Now, hastening back, they were panic-stricken by the discovery that the boat was in flames. It was also badly crushed, as though it had been lifted bodily and dropped on a ledge of sharp rocks. Worst of all, it contained the dead bodies of those who had been left on guard. The weapons of both men were missing, and they had been scalped but not otherwise mutilated.

Taking advantage of the confusion following this discovery, the Indian guide dove into a nearby thicket and disappeared. A minute later, while the whites were huddled about their burning boat attempting to extinguish the flames, a great flight of arrows, that seemed to come from every direction at once, instantly killed more than half their number. Then came a rush of yelling savages, and in another minute but one man was left alive. He was wounded, but his life had been spared by the express order of Massasoit.

The Indian guide had been made prisoner, bound, and left to himself; but now that all was over, the young leader, ordering his warriors to remain behind, went to him. Stooping, he severed the prisoner's bonds and assisted him to his feet. Then gazing steadily at him, he cried in a voice that trembled with emotion,—

"Tasquanto, my brother, dost thou not remember Massasoit?"

CHAPTER XXX

THE PILGRIMS OF PLYMOUTH

Since being separated from Massasoit years before in Plymouth harbor, Tasquanto, whose name the English had shortened to "Squanto," had known nothing of the fate of his fellow-captive beyond that he had been sold as a slave in London. In the mean time he had been received into the household of Sir Ferdinando Gorges, Governor of Plymouth, who had large interests in the New World, and had been taught to speak English. Then he was sent on trading-vessels to act as interpreter between whites and Indians. In this capacity he had made several voyages to America, but always so closely guarded that never until now had he been allowed to set foot on his native shores.

Tasquanto was so overcome at finding in the great sachem Massasoit, concerning whom he had heard much, his own long-lost friend that for a few moments he was speechless with joyful amazement. When he had succeeded in partially expressing this, he related briefly how he happened to be in his present situation, and added that the cruel taskmaster from whom he had just escaped was the same Captain Dermer who had formerly betrayed them into slavery.

"I knew it when first I saw him this morning," replied Massasoit, grimly, "for his evil face has ever been pictured in my heart. For that reason have I spared his worthless life until I could consult with thee, my brother, as to how we may best deal with him."

"Did you, then, know me also?" asked Tasquanto.

"The moment I set eyes on thee. Those white dogs had been slain an hour sooner but for thy presence among them and a fear of doing thee harm. Now, what say you? Shall this man be delivered to the tormentors, or shall he be killed where he lies? It is certain that his punishment must be great, for he has earned all that may be given. Also I do not care that he should recognize me and spread the report that I was once his slave, for that would shame me in the eyes of my people. Thou, too, must ever keep secret the matter of my having crossed the salt waters."

"I will remember," replied Tasquanto. "As for this white man, I would crop his ears with the same brand of ownership that he has placed upon many an Indian captured and sold into slavery. Then would I let him sail away in his own ship as a warning to all other white men. Death he deserves, since he has treated many of our people to death and worse, but to him the shame of cropped ears will be even more bitter than death."

So favorably was Massasoit impressed with this idea that he ordered it carried out at once. Thus, half an hour later, the brutal Dermer, who had done so much to cause the name of Englishman to be hated in the New World, was set adrift in a canoe, minus both his ears, and allowed to depart to his own ship. It is recorded in history that he reached Virginia, where he soon afterwards died from wounds received at the hands of New England savages.

Having thus satisfactorily concluded one part of his undertaking, Massasoit next turned his attention to the rebel Narragansetts. Moving his entire force against their stronghold, he demanded that all goods received from the English should be delivered up, and also that Miantinomo should come to his camp, bringing a chief's belt in token of submission. Massasoit swore that, in case his demands were refused, he would not depart from that place until every rebel in the fort was destroyed. So mild were these terms in comparison with what had been expected that they were instantly accepted, and a cruel war between neighbors was averted.

With peace thus restored, the authority of Massasoit over the great territory, already named New England by Captain John Smith, was so firmly established that until the day of his death it was never again questioned.

But if one of his two chief causes for anxiety was thus removed, the other was looming ominously near. Some six months after Tasquanto's escape from his long captivity a little English ship, buffeted by winter gales of the North Atlantic, was slowly approaching the American coast. Although only of one hundred and fifty tons' burden, or about the size of a small coasting schooner of to-day, she carried one hundred passengers besides her crew and an immense quantity of freight.

For three months had her passengers—men, women, and children—been on board the overcrowded little craft, and they were sick for a sight of land. Their destination was the mouth of the Shatemuc or Hudson River, but their first landfall, made under a cold December sky, was the bluff headland, stretching far out to sea like a beckoning finger, that Gosnold, some twenty years earlier, had named the Cape of Cods. From here the ship was headed southward towards her destination, but soon became involved in a labyrinth of shoals covered with roaring breakers. Also she was beaten by adverse gales until her weary company hailed with joy her captain's decision to run back to the safe shelter of Cape Cod. Here, in what is now the harbor of Provincetown, the sea-worn strangers disembarked, so profoundly happy at finding themselves once more on land that the wooded wilderness seemed a paradise.

They had come to establish homes in the New World, and though disappointed at not gaining the more southerly latitude for which they had set out, they now determined to remain where they were, since it was too late in the season for further explorations. Still, they spent two weeks in examination of the country close at hand, and finally selected a site for settlement across the bay enclosed by Cape Cod. Here was a good harbor, plenty of fresh water, and much land already cleared of forest growth by its former Indian occupants.

They named this place "Plymouth" after the last English port from which they had sailed, and on Christmas day began the work of building houses.

During that winter half of these stout-hearted settlers died, so that in the early spring only fifty persons, enfeebled by the sickness from which but seven had wholly escaped, remained to make good their claim to the land they had thus seized.

During all this time the colonists had not encountered any of the native owners of the soil, though they had caught occasional glimpses of vanishing forms, and often saw signal-fires or smokes that denoted the presence of watchful observers.

In spite of these things they did not hesitate to appropriate Indian property wherever they found it. Thus, when they discovered hidden stores of corn and parched acorns, laid by for winter use, they promptly removed them to Plymouth. Also whenever they ran across an Indian lodge, they took from it everything that seemed to them of value. They even robbed Indian graves of their sacred relics, and these things were reported to Massasoit by his scouts.

From the first appearance of the *Mayflower* on the stormy horizon he had known of all its movements. He had been relieved when it started southward, and was greatly disturbed by its return to Cape Cod. He was also much puzzled to account for the doings of its company, since evidently they were neither traders nor fishermen. Why had they brought women and children with them? Also why had they in the first place attempted to sail to the southward, if his country was the place they were seeking? He finally decided that they must be bound for the Virginia settlement of white men, and were only waiting until the winter storms were over before resuming their voyage to the country of Powhatan.

This decision eased Massasoit's mind, for, while he was determined that no whites should settle within his boundaries, he was also averse to unnecessary bloodshed. So he awaited patiently the departure that he believed the strangers would make with the coming of warmer weather. If they did not so depart, he knew that he could wipe them out of existence as easily as he could crush a worm that came in his path.

Thus forbearing to disturb them, he waited and watched, receiving almost daily reports from his scouts, who at all times lurked in the vicinity of the feeble settlement. He heard with grim satisfaction of their rapid decrease in numbers, and grew wroth at their violation of Indian graves and their appropriation of unguarded Indian property. Still he forbore to molest them, but as spring drew near he sent Samoset to learn how soon they intended to depart.

To his dismay this messenger brought back word that the English had no intention of ever again leaving the place where they had established themselves.

"Then must I remind them that I have no desire for their presence," quoth Massasoit, and at once he sent out runners to gather a large force of warriors in the vicinity of Plymouth. Accompanied by a body-guard of sixty men, the sachem himself hastened to the place of rendezvous and established a camp, from which he sent Tasquanto among the whites to learn in detail their strength and intentions.

With his ready command of English and his knowledge of white men's customs, gained by painful experience, Tasquanto or "Squanto," as he now called himself, found no difficulty in gaining all the information he desired from the strangers. He even learned their names and the relative rank held by their leading men.

When Tasquanto returned and reported these things, he mentioned one name that caused Massasoit to start and betray symptoms of great agitation.

"Art thou certain that one among them is so called?" he asked.

"I am certain," replied Tasquanto.

"Then go quickly and ask that man, as he values his own life and that of his people, to meet me alone by the big pine that looks down upon his lodges. I will be there unaccompanied. Stay! Take to him this belt that it may be to him a token of safe-conduct and true speaking."

With this Massasoit removed from his own person the great Belt of Seven Totems and handed it to Tasquanto. He also instructed the latter to withdraw beyond earshot when he had conducted the white man to the place of meeting.

Half an hour later Massasoit, with unpainted face and simply clad, stood alone at the foot of the great pine, looking down on the group of poor little huts that sheltered the feeble English remnant. Within a mile of the place were gathered five hundred warriors awaiting but a signal from him to utterly destroy the helpless settlement.

Then to him came an Englishman, young, sturdy, and heavily bearded. As he approached within a few paces he halted and examined the Indian curiously, for he had been told that he was to meet a sachem who was ruler of many tribes.

On the other hand, Massasoit gazed into the bearded face of the white man with an eagerness that was almost disconcerting. Then, as though satisfied with his scrutiny, he extended a hand, exclaiming as he did so,—

"Winslow! My frien' Winslow!"

For a moment the other hesitated, then his face lighted joyously as he grasped the proffered hand in both of his, crying,—

"Massasoit? They told me the name of the mighty chieftain was Massasoit, but never did I suspect that he was the friend whom I had found and lost in London."

For an hour the two, thus strangely brought together after years of distant wanderings, held converse with each other while the fate of the New World hung upon their words. When their conversation was finally ended, Winslow had promised never to reveal the fact that the proud sachem had once been bought and sold as a slave in England. He had also promised that the colony to which he belonged should never commit an act of aggression against the people of Massasoit, but that his friends should be their friends and his enemies their enemies.

On his part, and out of an abounding gratitude for the only friendship shown him at a time when he stood most in need of friends, Massasoit agreed that the poor little English settlement should be allowed to exist, and, moreover, promised to protect it from its enemies to the full extent of his power.

Then the two parted, the one to go back to his wondering warriors and dismiss them to their homes, the other to carry the glad news into Plymouth that the great Massasoit was ready to make a treaty of friendly alliance with his English neighbors.

So on the morrow Governor Carver, accompanied by Winslow, sturdy Myles Standish, and others of his principal men, met Massasoit. Then, after much feasting and an exchange of courtesies, they mutually signed a treaty of friendship that remained unbroken for upward of half a century from that memorable date.

Thus was the crumb of bread once cast upon troubled waters by Edward Winslow returned to him again with a thousand-fold of increase after many days.

Thus also did Nahma, son of Longfeather, now become Massasoit, wearer of the Belt of Seven Totems, make possible and establish forever the white man's settlement of New England.

* * * *

N. B. When the good ship *Mayflower* returned to England from that her most memorable voyage to the New World she bore in her cargo a packet of richest furs, together with many specimens of dainty beadwork, consigned to Lady Betty Effingham, who dwelt near to Bristol, England, with goodly wishes from her friend and humble servant, Massasoit.

www.ingramcontent.com/pod-product-compliance
Lightning Source LLC
Chambersburg PA
CBHW020143180626
46810CB00004B/1701